My Rebound

Special Edition

On My Own

Carrie Ann Ryan

MY REBOUND

An On My Own Novel

By
Carrie Ann Ryan

My Rebound
An On My Own Novel
By: Carrie Ann Ryan
© 2020 Carrie Ann Ryan

Cover Art by Wildfire Designs

Praise for Carrie Ann Ryan

"One of the best family romance series around! Carrie Ann Ryan brings the heat, emotions, and love in each story!" ~ NYT Bestselling Author Corinne Michaels

"Count on Carrie Ann Ryan for emotional, sexy, character driven stories that capture your heart!" – Carly Phillips, NY Times bestselling author

"Carrie Ann Ryan's romances are my newest addiction! The emotion in her books captures me from the very beginning. The hope and healing hold me close until the end. These love stories will simply sweep you away." ~ NYT Bestselling Author Deveny Perry

"Carrie Ann Ryan writes the perfect balance of sweet and heat ensuring every story feeds the soul." - Audrey Carlan, #1 New York Times Bestselling Author

"Carrie Ann Ryan never fails to draw readers in with passion, raw sensuality, and characters that pop off the page. Any book by Carrie Ann is an absolute treat." – New York Times Bestselling Author J. Kenner

"Carrie Ann Ryan knows how to pull your heartstrings and make your pulse pound! Her wonderful Redwood Pack series will draw you in and keep you reading long into the night. I can't wait to see what comes next with the new generation, the Talons. Keep them coming, Carrie Ann!" – Lara Adrian, New York Times bestselling author of CRAVE THE NIGHT

"With snarky humor, sizzling love scenes, and brilliant, imaginative worldbuilding, The Dante's Circle series reads as if Carrie Ann Ryan peeked at my personal wish list!" – NYT Bestselling Author, Larissa Ione

"Carrie Ann Ryan writes sexy shifters in a world full of passionate happily-ever-afters." – *New York Times* Bestselling Author Vivian Arend

"Carrie Ann's books are sexy with characters you can't help but love from page one. They are heat and heart blended to perfection." *New York Times* Bestselling Author Jayne Rylon

Carrie Ann Ryan's books are wickedly funny and deliciously hot, with plenty of twists to keep you guessing. They'll keep you up all night!" USA Today Bestselling Author Cari Quinn

"Once again, Carrie Ann Ryan knocks the Dante's Circle series out of the park. The queen of hot, sexy, enthralling paranormal romance, Carrie Ann is an author not to miss!" *New York Times* bestselling Author Marie Harte

MY REBOUND

A rebound isn't supposed to last. Though, sometimes, fate has other ideas in this opposites attract, friends with benefits romance.

It wasn't supposed to happen this way.

I started planning my future at the age of six. I knew the college I wanted, the career I needed, and the boy I would marry.

Only he wasn't supposed to break up with me in such a spectacular fashion. Now, I'm tossing my planner and breaking my rules.

First up: Pacey Ziglar.

I want one night of fun. One night to toss out all inhibitions with the sexy Brit across the hall. Too bad I fell for my rebound along the way.

I never meant to say yes.

I know exactly what Mackenzie Thomas wants when she asks me out on a date. She won't be my first no-strings-attached relationship, and if things work out the way we both want, she won't be my last.

Yet the more I get to know her, the more I want her. But she's not looking for me to be her forever.

And when my family secrets threaten our future, I'm afraid *forever* might end far too soon.

ONE

Mackenzie

THE START OF A NEW ADVENTURE SHOULD BE filled with anticipation, excitement, unease, and gut-churning tension. Perhaps not all of those emotions rolled into one, but that's how it felt at that moment with everything swirling around me, trying to dig in. I took a deep breath and looked at the two-story brownstone the girls and I were going to rent for the year. We had already signed our names to the lease and were about to move our belongings in to try and make the place our own.

I still couldn't quite believe this was happening.

"Why do you look like you're going to vomit?" Nessa asked as she stood by me.

I sighed. "Oh, no reason."

"You shouldn't be worried," the other girl said with a sly

smile. "We don't bite. At least, I don't think we do. Maybe Natalie does."

"Why am I the biter of the group?" Natalie asked, chuckling. "If anybody, it's you."

"She has you there," Elise added, her eyes dancing with laughter. I looked at the three girls I would be living with for the foreseeable future and smiled. They had lived together for the past couple of years in another home they knew they could never go back to, thanks to circumstances that had broken all of us in different ways. Together, they had connections, memories, and so much hope and love. I was the outsider, but I was going to make this work. I had a plan, a to-do list, and the ability to place checkmarks on that plan. I could make things work.

"Seriously, though, why do you look so nervous?" Nessa asked, the humor in her voice gone, now replaced by worry.

I smiled, hoping it reached my eyes. "This is my first time living with you guys. I hope you don't mind my eccentric ways."

Elise met my gaze. I saw the sadness there, but I ignored it. Because I had to. I was the replacement. There had been another girl, another roommate, a friend we loved. But Corinne wasn't here anymore, and that was the reason the ladies couldn't go back to their old home. The reason we were all moving to another house together rather than me merely moving into their already well-maintained place.

"As long as you don't leave wet towels on the floor, I'm sure we can make do," Natalie said.

I shuddered. "Why on earth would you ever think I would leave a wet towel on the floor?"

Natalie grinned. "I know, even saying that made me cringe."

"As it should," I replied. "If anything, my chore wheel will probably annoy you. I'm not going to be the one leaving messes behind." Elise and Nessa met each other's gazes before they broke out into laughter.

I blushed, ducking my head against the cool wind that came from the lovely January breeze in Denver, Colorado.

"What?" I asked, worried I'd crossed a line.

"Oh, it's just I owe Elise ten bucks," Nessa said, grinning.

I flushed, and it wasn't only from the cold. "I'm sorry?"

Elise pushed at Nessa's shoulder. "I thought you would bring up the chore wheel before we even walked in the door. She assumed you'd wait until after we'd unpacked."

I felt the blush creep up my neck. "I'm sorry, I had one with my other roommates. Is that not what you guys do? Oh, crap. We don't have to do anything like that here. You tell me what to do, and I'll do it."

Natalie squeezed my hand, and I smiled at the other woman. I had met the girls through Natalie. We had been study partners for her class, and I had easily fit in with the crew. Now, I felt like I was off-kilter because I wasn't just the friend who came over but one who would be living with them. Without Corinne.

"No, we like chore wheels," Elise said. Then she shuddered. "Okay, not really *like*, but we use them. That way, we can get things done. We all like a clean house. You're going to fit in just fine, Mackenzie. Stop worrying."

"You clearly don't know me that well if you're telling me I shouldn't worry. It's sort of my thing."

They laughed and then clasped hands, Nessa reaching out to grip one of mine, Natalie the other.

I felt something spark within me, a connection forming that I hadn't expected. Or rather, I hadn't wanted to expect.

I liked these women. They were my friends. I could do this. I just needed to find my place within their system. There were places and boxes for everybody. Rules and connections and paths. I did my best when I knew the equation and the answer and everything that came with it. I just needed to find where I belonged.

"Are we just going to stand out here all day and look at the place? Or are you actually going to walk in?"

I winced and looked behind me at the four guys who stood by the moving truck and their vehicles, their arms folded across their chests.

"Hello, boys," I said, and they all smiled. I swore my knees went weak, even though I told myself I didn't want a guy—ever again. Not after the last one. But I couldn't help it. The boys from the house on college row were handsome, swoon-worthy, and easily made your knees go weak every time you looked at them. All four of them staring at you with a smile on their faces? It was no wonder my heart raced.

There used to be five of them. But unlike what'd happened with the girls, the split hadn't been tragic. Maybe a little for me at first, but it wasn't a tragedy. It was a farce.

But I wasn't going to think about Sanders. He wasn't living with the guys anymore, which meant I wouldn't let him have real estate in my mind or my heart, either.

He'd occupied enough of it since we were infants. I wouldn't let him be there now.

Dillon, Elise's boyfriend, cleared his throat as he walked

forward. "The cold front's coming in. That means we're probably going to get snow or ice soon. Let's get you guys at least unpacked and into the house where it's warm. The place does have heat, right?"

He looked at the home dubiously, and I sighed. "Of course," I said. "Do you think we'd find a place that doesn't have heat? The four of us? We're smarter than that."

"But you had to find a place at the last minute," Pacey said, and I ignored him. I had to do that often. He was my friend, but sometimes that British accent did things to me that I'd rather not think about. I'd always been drawn to him as a friend, even when I was with Sanders. Now, it felt as if things were weird. They were all a little strained with me. What were you supposed to do around the girl who had only become your friend because she was dating a former roommate? Their roommate wasn't there anymore, but I was still around.

What was I supposed to do?

What were *they* supposed to do?

Elise clapped her hands, bringing me out of my thoughts. "Come on, let's get the boxes inside."

"I suppose we'll need to be the ones to move the furniture?" Tanner asked from the side, his voice low. He never did anything quickly, never shouted—except for that one time. I had never seen him move as fast as he had when he punched Sanders and then kept beating him. Sanders had fought back, and both of them had ended up with bloody lips and bruised eyes, but Tanner hadn't said a thing to me afterward. He'd barely even looked at me since I'd walked in on Sanders getting a blowjob from a girl I didn't even know.

I pushed those thoughts from my mind and closed my

eyes, counting to ten. I needed to focus on the now, on the future. I had a future planned. That was me. What I was known for. This semester would be amazing. I had classes that mattered and a program I would begin over the summer that I needed to plan for and make sure my grades were ready for. I had a path. I just needed to focus on that and not on my personal life.

Except for the fact that I kind of missed the whole relationship and sex thing. I wasn't going to think about that, though. Because I didn't need it. Not everybody needed an emotional connection or even a physical one. They lived their lives perfectly without any of that. I could be one of those people.

At least, I hoped.

"Okay, let's get this done," Dillon said, and then he whistled through his fingers.

"Did you just whistle?" Nessa asked, and Dillon shrugged, blushing.

"He's like that. Positively annoying," Pacey said and grinned down at Nessa.

Miles, the final roommate, simply shrugged. "Well, it got our attention, didn't it?"

"We should get going. I have a list." I pulled out my tablet and clipboard. "And I have assignments if you'll let me."

"You have a list? Shocking," Pacey said as he came over to me.

I raised a brow. "Are you making fun of me?"

"I would never make fun of you, darling."

I narrowed my eyes. "I feel like that's a lie."

"Perhaps. But I'm not making fun of you right now.

How's that? Now, for real, give us our assignments before I freeze my bollocks off."

I snorted and then did my best not to think about Pacey like that. Sometimes, I couldn't help it, though. He was all blond and blue-eyed...and British. It was a little too much with the alliteration of sexiness. I did my best not to think about guys at all like that anymore. It'd only been five weeks since I walked in on Sanders and that girl. And I had been with Sanders since the cradle, as we all joked. In reality, we had been in middle school when we started dating, and we hadn't dated anyone else since. At least, that's what I had thought. As it turned out, Sanders had figured that blowjobs and whatever the hell else he was doing didn't count as cheating. He was wrong, and so, here I was, alone and on a new path. But that was fine. I would find what worked for me even if I wanted to throw up in the end.

I pushed those thoughts away and looked down at my notes. "I do have assignments."

"We're here," Tanner said. "And I'm about to freeze my balls off, not my bollocks."

"Whatever words you boys think you need to use, that's what we're going to freeze off." Pacey waved him off.

I shook my head, ignoring the two of them as they continued talking about balls. *Guys.* I gave out everyone's assignments. They nodded, and we got busy. It was heavy work, strenuous, and soon, no one was freezing anymore. We were all sweaty and trying to ignore the chill.

By the time we got the furniture in and set up, I was glad that I had ordered in lunch. We had Chinese food delivered for everybody and dove in while still unpacking some boxes. We wouldn't get to everything tonight, and I didn't expect the guys to help us with that, but they were great at reaching things that we couldn't.

They moved in couches, beds, and all the other random, assorted furniture we had gathered over time. Most of it was Natalie's. Her family had furnished the house they'd lived in prior, and they had most everything they needed, though Natalie didn't like to talk about it. Considering I enjoyed sitting on the couch instead of on the living room floor, I didn't mind. The set was comfortable, made well, and I had a feeling far more expensive than anything I could afford.

"Okay, lunch is over. Let's get back to it," Miles announced and blushed as we all stared at him.

"Look at you, taking the reins," Pacey said, and the other guy flipped him off.

"I can take the reins just fine, Pacey. I just tend to be quieter than the rest of you."

"I don't know, Miles, if you're going to be taking control like this, I should be on my knees or something," Tanner said, and I groaned as the girls threw some throw pillows at them.

I looked over at Pacey, who sat next to me on the couch, and shook my head. "How many sex jokes do you think we go through a day?" I asked.

Pacey raised a brow. "Probably far more than you even realize. But we're guys. It's what we do."

"You say that as if girls don't make as many sex jokes as you do."

"Oh, really? You should tell me then. I'll let you know if they're dirty or not."

My stomach tightened. "Are you flirting with me, Pacey?"

"Maybe. It is the way of my namesake, after all."

I frowned. "Who were you named after?"

"The dreamboat from *Dawson's Creek*, of course," he drawled.

"Wait. But you're British. I didn't know it was a huge thing over there." Not that I knew anything about what was popular in the UK in the late nineties and early two-thousands.

"My mother was an American teenager during the heyday of Dawson and Pacey."

"Oh, wow. I didn't realize the show was that old."

"Please never mention that to my mother. She will hurt me for telling you the story."

I laughed. "Deal."

We got to work again fairly quickly, cleaning up our mess and continuing to put things on walls as we unpacked. While I had it in my mind that we would get a lot done today, I hadn't honestly expected the guys to stay for as long as they did. I was grateful, yet I wasn't sure how we would be able to repay them.

I ended up in the office area, a small nook with a bay window and four small desks that we could make into a study library, and found myself alone with Pacey.

"You need to stop looking like that."

I frowned, taking in my jeans with holes and the bright red leggings peeking through. It was cold, but I still wanted to be somewhat fashionable. I had on a cream-colored sweater that had seen better days, but it was perfect for moving day and was off-the-shoulder and layered with a long-sleeved shirt and two tank tops underneath. The house had decent heating and quality insulation, but I was still cold, even with all the moving around. Hence, the layering. I had piled my dark hair on the top of my head and long since sweated off any concealer and powder I'd had on earlier.

"How do you think I'm looking?" I asked, a little weary.

Pacey cursed under his breath, that accent of his doing things to me I'd rather not think about. I didn't want a guy, at least that's what I kept telling myself. But there was just something about Pacey. Probably because he was safe. He didn't want a long relationship, and he was straightforward about it with everybody he was with. He also wasn't sure if he would stay in the States after he graduated, and there was no way people wanted to do that whole long-distance thing. He would be great for someone who desired something short-term. And I wasn't sure I wanted anything when and if I found myself ready to date again. But he was safe to pretend with, smile with, and think about. Especially that accent. But nothing else.

Pacey Ziglar wasn't safe in the slightest when it came to most other things.

"I was saying that you have a look on your face. I didn't mean what you're dressed in. You look lovely."

I raised a brow and looked at his sculpted Henley and jeans that didn't have a speck of dirt on them, even though we had been unpacking all day. "You say that, and yet I feel judged."

"I could go down on bended knee in awe about your gorgeousness, your beauty, and your aura of peace, but I'm afraid you wouldn't believe me."

"Because I wouldn't. But what were you talking about just then? What look?"

"The one on your face. The one that says you're going to

need to think about how to repay us other than with Chinese food that we all split, in case you forgot."

"You did what?"

"Dillon made sure we all split the bill."

"I should've known I needed to take care of that ahead of time. Natalie and I had a plan."

"And while that was wonderful, the guys and I ate twice as much as any of you. Though I am glad that you all decided to eat rather than move food around on your plates and pretend."

I rolled my eyes. "We needed the calories. I'm not going to eat a salad or air and pretend that I'm perfectly fine not eating. But I'm going off the subject here. You guys shouldn't have paid for that. The girls and I wanted to pay. That way, it was sort of a thank you. Just not the complete payment because you guys have done so much work. Way beyond the scope of even my plans."

Pacey gave me a pointed look and glanced at the planner in my hand. "How much of this was in your plans?"

"I may have color-coded some things, but I assumed you guys would be home by now. Seriously, though, thank you. I don't know how we're going to repay you." Pacey lifted a brow, and I blushed. "Not that. Well, maybe Elise. So, Dillon will get paid. But, sadly, I don't think the rest of you guys will."

Pacey threw back his head and laughed, and I ignored the way his throat worked, how his blond hair moved away from his face as he smiled.

There was just something about Pacey, and he annoyed me. At least, that's what I kept telling myself. After all, I was the girl on the rebound—or whatever other titles I wanted to give it. I didn't think I was over Sanders, although I might be. I wasn't sure. And I wasn't going to think about it, so there was no way I would let myself fall for the drama and beauty that was Pacey. I knew he believed in forevers because he'd talked about it with Dillon and Elise. But he wouldn't be *my* forever.

"So, Mackenzie. What else is in your planner?" he whispered, his voice low. We were alone on this side of the house, the others all in the bedrooms or the living room area. Tanner was in the kitchen, organizing it for us, and I let him. Mostly because Natalie and I would reorganize it if we needed to. But Tanner seemed to know what he was doing, and I had to give him credit for that.

"What do you mean?"

"You keep looking at me. I want to know why."

"No reason," I said, lifting my chin even though I knew my cheeks were red.

"Mackenzie, you can talk to me. We're mates. Aren't we?"

I swallowed hard. "I don't know," I said honestly, and his eyes widened in surprise. "I'm sorry. But I knew you guys through Sanders. I mean, I met Natalie in school, but I honestly don't know if we would've become as close if Elise hadn't been dating Dillon. And it all just melded together. And now that I'm not with Sanders anymore, it's just weird."

"It would've been weird if you had taken his room—though it's still empty if this doesn't work out." He winked, and I rolled my eyes.

"I'm not moving in with a bunch of boys."

"Your loss," he drawled, leaning against the doorway. He

looked over his shoulder, then moved into the room, closing the door behind him. My eyebrows winged up.

"What was that for?"

"So we can have some privacy—not for what you're thinking," he amended. "Talk to me, Mackenzie. What's wrong?"

I shrugged and looked down at the boxes around me. "There's just a lot to do. This year, I have to prep for my internship and the program for my thesis. It's the last semester of our junior year. Things ramp up."

"You're right, they do. But you weren't thinking about any of that just now."

"What am I supposed to think? I had my entire life planned out in front of me, Pacey. You all made fun of me enough for it that you know that. And now, all of that's been thrown out the window because Sanders wanted a blowjob from another girl just to see how it felt. He needed to take notes and describe it to himself so he could compare it to us."

My blood boiled, and Pacey just shook his head and took a step forward. He was in my space then, and I swallowed hard. He tucked a stray strand of hair behind my ear and leaned down, resting his forehead on mine. I froze, wondering what the hell he was doing. We were not this close. I didn't even think Pacey liked me all that much. I was usually the loud, annoying one who made lists. And now, here he was, touching me.

And I had no idea what the hell he was doing.

"Mackenzie, breathe."

"It's tough to do when you're touching me. Mostly because I'm not a huge fan of people touching me. And you're really close." I said the words quickly, and he let out a rough chuckle before stepping back, leaving the scent of sandalwood and something that was all Pacey behind.

What the hell was going on?

"Sanders, or *Paul* like I like to call him in my head now because that is his name and he doesn't get to have the suave nickname—"

"He always hated that name as a kid."

"Well, now he doesn't get to have a nice name. One he likes. I'll call him Paul. Just for you. And for me, because he annoyed me."

"Thank you?" I asked, and Pacey's lips twitched.

"You're welcome." He paused. "Talk to me, Mackenzie. What else is on your mind?"

I looked at him and thought... *Why not*? Why couldn't I just tell him what was on my mind, blurt it out, get embarrassed, and never see him again? After all, I wouldn't be hanging out with the guys as much anymore. Or ever. While their house was larger, a lot nicer, and Elise would likely go over there, I could stay here. Right?

"I have a lot of things in my plan for the year. And part of that was to have sex—at least when I was with Sanders. Because I like sex. I like relationships. And now, I don't know what not having that means for my future. But I know that to get through my checklist of who I need to be, I need a rebound. I have to get out there and somehow find that next step so people can stop thinking about Sanders when they look at me and give me those pitying looks. Even with classes and school and moving into a new home with roommates who don't really know me. I need to find a rebound. So,

Pacey, what do you think? Do you think you can find one for me?"

I knew the sarcasm dripping from my tone at that point was ridiculous, but he had asked. And my plan was even more ridiculous-sounding when said out loud.

Pacey just blinked, raised a brow, and smiled. "Well, Mackenzie, I thought you'd never ask."

"What the hell do you mean by that?" I asked, a little afraid I knew precisely what he was thinking.

"You're looking for a rebound? Well, darling, you're looking right at him."

Two

Pacey

As soon as the words left my lips, some part of me knew they were a mistake. Only when it came to Mackenzie Thomas, I couldn't regret the offer. The look on her face etched itself into my mind. She hadn't said no, hadn't blinked or walked away. She hadn't screamed or slapped me or called me vicious names. Instead, she had squinted at me, confusion written on her face even as I knew an idea sparked behind those wide and expressive hazel eyes. But before she could say anything, before I could even explain why I had offered myself up as her next bedroom rebound or any other word she preferred to use for the occasion, the door opened behind me. The moment shared between us was broken.

At least in that instance.

Miles came in, a brow raised, and simply shook his head before bringing another box into the fray. Others joined, and we went through the business of helping the girls unpack. I stayed for another hour, though Mackenzie hadn't been alone with me. I would've thought it odd, but she was rarely alone with me. After all, she had been my roommate's girlfriend, the one we had all assumed he would marry someday. And yet, that hadn't happened. Paul Sanders had decided to ruin it all by having sex with another girl. Oh, you could call a blowjob by any number of other names, but having someone's mouth around your dick while your girlfriend was downstairs cleaning up your party mess? I called that sex. Cheating.

Anything that could break someone's heart like that was beyond a simple shaking of hands. It was sharing bodily fluids in ways I did not want to imagine. But sadly, I knew what Paul's dick looked like now because he hadn't bothered to finish tucking himself back into his boxers when Tanner and I walked in behind Mackenzie, trying to help—or at least attempting to see what we could do. Sanders had blustered, and Tanner had taken care of him. On the other hand, I had pushed the man from my mind the moment I saw him cheating.

If I had known what had been going on behind his closed door, I wouldn't have let Mackenzie walk in there. Some people might think I was the spider on the web, making sure that everybody adhered to my wishes, but that was far from the case. I never wanted Mackenzie to be hurt. And if I'd had any inkling that Sanders had gone beyond mere flirting with other women, I would have told her. At first, I had thought Sanders was acting like a jerk, puffing himself up because he was the big man on campus. I hadn't known it had gone beyond a casual smile or a joke shared between friends. If I had, I would have done something about it. Not for Sanders, but for Mackenzie. Because she was a good person and didn't deserve what the wanker had done to her.

I hadn't seen it and had been too late. But I had been the one to tell her to keep her chin up and pretend that it didn't hurt.

Only I knew it had to hurt. Things that twisted you up deep inside always did. And Mackenzie seemed the sort to need things in perfect little piles or little boxes that sat on shelves, waiting to be unpacked for the next instance. And her entire shelf had tumbled from the wall.

Would I be her rebound? I didn't know. Did she even want one? I honestly didn't think so. But I would throw myself on the proverbial sword to make a girl I respected smile.

Maybe that was callous of me, at least in some people's eyes, but I didn't care. Mackenzie needed someone to talk to, that much was clear, and I wouldn't mind lending an ear. At least until she found the new track she needed to be on. Then, she would walk away, and I would find my next chance to live life. As I had learned early on, life wasn't worth living if you didn't take those chances. Or maybe, life was simply far too short—or any other metaphor about life and living you could think of.

I knew I would see Mackenzie soon, and I wouldn't let her forget the question she had asked and the offer I had made, if only to see her cheeks blush.

"Pacey, are you not paying attention?" my mother inquired. I blinked, pulling myself back into the moment.

"I'm sorry, I was lost in thought."

"Clearly. School, I hope?" Mum asked.

I nodded, lying. "Pretty much. The semester's about to begin, so I don't have studies on my mind per se, but classes nonetheless."

"You sure do like adding extra words when you don't need them," my mother said, rolling her eyes.

I smiled, knowing it was a joke between us. I liked to sound my most pompous in front of my dad, mostly because he was far more snobbish than I could ever be. My parents had met when they were far too young, and my mother had gotten pregnant with dear old me. I hadn't had any say in the matter, of course, but I had ended up being born outside of London, where we had lived for most of my life. My parents had moved me across the pond ten years ago to finish university in America—where my mother was from—and I hadn't really understood it at the time. I still didn't, but we were closer to her family, and I didn't mind having a connection to both sides of my world. I just didn't know where I would go after school. Would I go back to the UK, where my father's family was? Where my parents still spent half their time? Or would I stay here near my mother's family, finding my place in a country where my accent wasn't too familiar, and people thought I was interesting? I tended to blend in back in my home country, at least that's what I told myself. My mother said that could never happen, but that was mothers for you. They always thought the best of their children.

Honestly, I wasn't sure I wanted to go back to my first home where the walls still spoke, and everything seemed so dreary. Not because of the weather or the people, but from the memories that never seemed to fade away.

Wow. I was far too melancholic for my own good today.

"I don't understand why we're here. You can never get a decent cuppa in Denver," my father grumbled, looking down at his teacup. His lips twitched in a smile as he said it, the refrain familiar.

I had added a splash of milk to mine, just to see what my father would do. I liked tea any way I could get it, but if anybody touched my cup and put it near a microwave, I would never forgive them. There were electric tea kettles for a reason. If you couldn't use a teapot on a stove, find a tea kettle.

That was one thing I never understood about Americans.

"Anyway, darling," my mother said, smiling. She had kept her American accent, and since she was in Colorado, she always said that she had no accent as that was the epitome of being a Coloradan. I hadn't understood until I moved here and spoke to the locals. But every once in a while, she added a bit of a twist at the end of her vowels and consonants and sounded more like my father's sister, with a touch of an accent. I loved her so freaking much. I just wished that I got to see her more often.

"Your mother and I asked you to dinner while we were in town to talk to you." I looked at my dad and then at my mom, frowning. We usually went out to tea when they were in town since they spent most of their time at the London house these days, but something about my dad's tone worried me.

"What's wrong?"

"Your father and I..." my mother began and then cleared her throat.

She gave my father a pointed look, and he sighed.

"Your mother and I have decided to get a divorce. We feel it's the best thing for both of us, and we wanted to let you know in person rather than have you hear about it from someone else."

I blinked and looked between them, confused. "What?"

"No need to raise your voice, son," my father said before he lowered his. "We probably should've done this at home, but we always go out to tea when we're in town, and we didn't want you to worry."

I looked between them and swallowed hard before looking down at my teacup. My chest constricted, and I tried to keep up. My parents seemed the epitome of happiness. They were the reason I knew that marriage could work, even though most of my friends had parents who were divorced. It didn't make any sense. "You're saying this, just like that? After how many years of marriage? You're just ending it?"

"Your father and I had twenty years," Mum said. "It's time for us to move on in our journeys." There was something she wasn't saying. I saw it in her eyes, but she didn't want me to make a scene. God forbid we made a fucking scene. My parents were getting a divorce. It wasn't like I even lived with them. I had my own life, a home. But what the hell?

"I didn't even know you guys were fighting."

My mother smiled softly, but it still didn't reach her eyes. What had I missed? After all these years, what wasn't I seeing?

My father let out a breath. "There are some things you don't let your children see, Pacey."

"We want you to know that we love you. We always have,

and we always will. No matter what happens between your father and me, you will always be our number one priority. You may be an adult, but you are still our son." She looked over at my dad. "Right, Edward?"

"Yes, Penelope. Pacey is our number one. And whatever you decide, Pacey—at least for yourself in the future—know we'll both be with you. We just won't be together."

They kept talking, and I blinked, wondering how the hell this had happened. They had been through so much. They had been young when they got married and had dealt with clashing cultures and families that hadn't understood their love. They had weathered my countless hospitalizations —and still did, for that matter. Yet they had stayed together. They had only grown stronger. What the hell had I missed when I moved out?

But I knew this wasn't the time or place to question it further. Instead, my father raised his fingers in a slight gesture, and the waiter came with our check. It didn't matter that we were at one of the most coveted and elite places for afternoon tea in Denver. I just wanted to scream and try to figure this out. But I wasn't going to get that. Because I wasn't allowed to question. That wasn't what sons did. They listened to their parents and they nodded. They did as they were told. They did not scream or fight or wonder why the hell their parents were getting a divorce after so many years. Why the hell hadn't I known anything?

"I can see that you're confused, and we'll talk about it soon. But right now, we must go. I know you have school starting tomorrow morning. We don't want to keep you."

"Mum," I whispered.

"Another time, Pacey." My mother squeezed my hand,

and then we got up from the table and walked towards the front of the building where the valet was.

"I'm headed to my hotel," my father said, and I blinked.

"You're not staying with Aunt Tracy?" I asked.

My mother blushed. "I am, Pacey. Your father will be staying at a hotel. But we're here for you. I promise." She kissed my cheek and then walked away, my father nodding after he squeezed my shoulder. They left me alone, standing there wondering how on earth this had happened. And what was I supposed to do about it?

I drove home, rubbing my temple as I did. I could feel a migraine coming on, but I hoped it was only a stress headache. I needed to drink more water, and since I was usually on a schedule when it came to hydrating, I was annoyed with myself for not doing better. I was just a little off. Had been since losing Corinne. I winced as I turned off the highway near the campus. I didn't want to think about her. She had been a nice girl and was taken from us much too soon. How could a brain aneurysm steal a girl so full of life? And so quickly? We hadn't even had a proper chance to say goodbye. She was suddenly gone, leaving us all wondering what the hell had happened.

Stress usually exacerbated my condition, even though I did my best to stay on top of everyday routines. Only I hadn't been lately, and that was on me. I would have to focus on what I *could* change. And that was to work on my studies, drink water as I should, and pretend like I didn't have a care in the world. Because that was what I was known for, being laid-back. And that's what I would keep doing.

Even if it potentially killed me.

I winced at that thought and pulled into the garage

behind the home where I lived with three of my friends. At one point, there had been a fifth, but Sanders was no more. And though he would still roam the campus halls and lurk around unsuspecting girls, I didn't have to have him in my house anymore, at least.

After Tanner had beaten him in that fight, Sanders had told everybody that he didn't want to be in the same room with a bruiser and then left. We all knew it was because Sanders wanted nothing to do with us anymore once we took Mackenzie's side. We wanted nothing to do with him, either. Dillon, Tanner, Miles, and I weren't sorry he was gone. Our landlord and benefactor had been nice about not increasing our rent after Sanders left, and maybe one day, we would add another roommate. But for now, the current dynamic worked. Sanders had always been slightly different from the other guys anyway, probably because the kid always seemed to land on his feet no matter where he went or what happened. He was currently living with his brother, and his parents were working on getting him a flat.

I didn't care what he did. I didn't put much thought into what most kids did, as long as they didn't do it near me.

I walked into the house, grabbed my water from the fridge, and headed to my room. Dillon and Elise were in the living room, talking about their course load for the next day. I figured they'd go up to Dillon's room later and enjoy their evening. I could hear Miles behind his door, talking on the phone to someone. Probably his parents, wondering exactly what he had done for the day and if he'd eaten his vegetables.

I didn't see Tanner anywhere, but he could be brooding in a corner for all I knew. My friends might joke that I saw all and knew all. I just happened to be more observant than most. At least, I liked to think so.

I closed the door behind me, popped an ibuprofen, and lay down on my bed after I took a big gulp of water.

My head hurt, but that would go away soon. At least, I hoped. My heart, though? I didn't know what to do with that.

My parents had loved each other. They were the epitome of what I thought romance should be. They were together through the good times, the hard times, and the unbearable times.

And now, all of a sudden, they weren't together anymore.

My father might be a little stuck-up and overbearing at times, but he also smiled and laughed and taught me to play chess with a grin on his face and his heart on his sleeve.

And yet, my parents didn't love each other anymore. What the hell was I supposed to do with that?

Falling out of love unexpectedly seemed to be a recent occurrence, which reminded me of Mackenzie. I pulled my phone out of my pocket and looked down at the screen. I settled onto my pillows a bit so I was sitting up, took another sip of my water, and figured I might as well keep stirring the pot. Mackenzie needed a friend, and I had a feeling that while her new roommates might be trying to make sure she was part of their crew, she still felt off. Distant. I couldn't blame her for that. It was an odd situation—Corinne being gone, and Mackenzie moving in. It might be a new house for them all, but there were distinct layers there that I wasn't sure everybody realized they had waded into.

Mackenzie needed a friend. And hell, maybe I did, too.

Me: *Did you think about my offer?*

I grinned, imagining her scowling at her phone as she looked down at it. Either that or she'd toss it against the wall and pretend I hadn't texted at all.

Mackenzie: *Not at all. I have some things to worry about. Like meetings with my advisor and school. And all the syllabuses or syllabi that I have to read.*

I grinned.

Me: *I think you're lying.*

Mackenzie: *I think you are too cocky for your own good.*

I laughed.

Me: *Maybe. I can't help it. It's just me.*

I tried not to think about the fact that she had used the word *cock* in a sentence. I did my best to ignore it. I wasn't flirting with her to flirt with her. I was trying to make her smile. I couldn't want her that way. I didn't do serious, and Mackenzie was all about the serious. I only wanted to make her smile. Because I knew that she missed that.

Mackenzie: *You're incorrigible then. And no, I haven't thought about your offer.*

Me: *And that's another lie.*

She was silent for so long I was afraid she really had thrown her phone.

Mackenzie: *Fine, it was a lie. Why would you say something like that? Why would you offer?*

Me: *Because, my darling Mackenzie, a rebound doesn't need to be defined by what society says it is. It can be whatever you need it to be.*

Mackenzie: *I don't understand you.*

Me: *Nobody ever does. Go on a date with me, Mackenzie.*

Show the world that you bounced back, are happy, and are ready to worry about your journey and not what they think.

Mackenzie: *So, you're saying you want to be my rebound for other people?*

Me: *No, I want to be your rebound because I don't want you to worry about other people.*

Mackenzie: *I don't understand you, Pacey.*

I smiled, knowing she was repeating herself.

Me: *You don't need to. Just think about it.*

Mackenzie: *I have class tomorrow. So do you. And you know damn well I'll be thinking about it.*

I smiled and drank more of my water.

Me: *Good, my plan is complete. Sleep well, Mackenzie. And think and dream about me.*

Mackenzie: *Not even in the slightest, Pace.*

I smiled at the nickname.

Me: *But I've planted the seed in your head. You won't be able to resist me.*

Mackenzie: *You annoy me. I'll see you in class. I hate you.*

Me: *You don't. That's why you're thinking about me. Your favorite rebound.*

I set down the phone, knowing she wouldn't text again. I would see her in class tomorrow, and then I'd determine what to do. Because I knew that even through her scowl, a smile would appear.

And maybe, just maybe, the semester wouldn't be so terrible, after all.

THREE

Mackenzie

"HOW DO WE ALREADY HAVE SO MUCH WORK? IT'S only been a week."

I looked up at Nessa and smiled. "Because it's college, and they're all trying to outdo one another," I replied snarkily, and Nessa just rolled her eyes.

"At least you like your classes. I'm still trying to figure out if I even like my major."

I shook my head. "You do. This semester is just different."

"I think I tell myself that every semester. Say I'll get used to it. But then I find myself wanting to watch Netflix and drink tea and pretend that I don't have to do anything, and money just comes to me."

"That's the dream," Natalie added as she frowned over

her textbook. Elise sat on the other end of the couch, a frown on her face as she looked at her syllabus. I sighed, knowing that while the rest of them could probably do some of their coursework online, I had a paper that I could try to focus on, but I had proofs that needed to be done first and on paper. That's what happened when you were a math major.

"I like math." I shrugged and thought back on Nessa's words. "Tea? I thought you drank coffee."

"Oh," she said, blushing. "Pacey got me hooked on tea. Now, I can't stop drinking it. He bought me this awesome Harney & Sons blend. It's called Paris, and it's fruity and yummy."

Natalie leaned forward. "You like fruity tea? I thought you liked sweet black tea."

Nessa just smiled. "Oh, it's not like a fruit tea like hibiscus or anything, more like a black tea with a hint of sweet flavor. He also has a chocolate one, but he won't let me have any."

"Chocolate tea?" I asked, intrigued. "That sounds marvelous."

"It is," Nessa said dreamily, leaning into the couch.

"Tea," I muttered. "Maybe it'll be better than coffee and will still keep me up this semester."

"I don't know, I like coffee," Elise said, smiling softly into her book.

I met Natalie's gaze, and we both smiled.

"I know why you like coffee," Nessa teased.

"Oh, shush," Elise said and sank into her end of the couch.

She had met Dillon for the first time in a coffee shop,

though they hadn't spoken. No, a dare at a house party had begun their genuine relationship. But that fated meeting across the way at that coffee shop, the place we all went to and loved that was three stories and full of spaces to study, was their meet-cute. At least, according to them. And they frequently went there and met up during the day if their classes weren't on opposite ends of campus.

It was my favorite place to study if I wasn't at home, as well. It had just the right number of people to get my extrovert fix, but not enough that it was too loud and annoying and I couldn't study.

I didn't know if I considered myself an extrovert or an omnivert. I sort of got exhausted after a while no matter what, but I usually blamed that on me. Because I had to be the one helping out, cleaning up, and making sure things ran smoothly—even at parties that weren't mine. I had done it repeatedly last semester for Sanders and his roommates. I let my thoughts fade off after that and then cursed at myself.

It sucked that I didn't have that anymore but was I upset because I didn't have Sanders, or that I didn't have that connection?

Maybe I could have that with Pacey. Not everything I had with Sanders, but at least a connection to the guys. No, that would be wrong. Just because Pacey offered himself up as a rebound didn't mean I had to take him up on the offer.

Though I was pretty sure I had in a text last week.

And in the once since when he just asked how school was going. It had been nice. I had a friend.

And yet, I had no idea what would happen next. That should worry me. I always knew what was going to happen next. I had plans and checkboxes for all of that. Of course, I hadn't known what would happen before, but I had been delusional when it came to Sanders.

There was something terribly wrong with me, and I didn't want to think about it anymore.

"What is that face you're making?" Natalie asked, tilting her head as she looked at me.

I blushed. "Nothing. Everything's fine."

"Well, that's a lie," Nessa countered.

I sighed. "No, it's not."

"You're not fine. And you haven't talked about what happened last month," Natalie whispered.

I froze and looked around, noticing that Elise had gone still, as well.

Natalie closed her eyes and let out a tiny little curse. "I'm sorry. I didn't mean *everything* that happened last month. I'm so sorry."

Elise waved it off and wiped at a tear. "No, Corinne is bound to come up often. After all, she lived with all of us for so long." She winced. "Well, she was *friends* with all of us anyway."

I smiled softly, ignoring the odd hurt that took root when it shouldn't. I hadn't been their roommate before. I needed to get my head out of my ass and focus on what I could fix, what I could feel without regret.

"You're talking about Sanders," I said, using my pain to change the conversation. I didn't want the girls focusing on Corinne's memory just then, not when I knew they were still hurting.

So, I did the best that I could.

"We can talk about him if you'd like," Natalie said. "I know he was a huge part of your life."

I shook my head, my stomach roiling. "And he's not anymore. He can do whatever he wants, though I'm sure I'll see him around campus. Thank God I don't have any classes with him this semester."

I had classes with his friends, though. Ones that snickered and tried to act as if they hadn't known me for the past two years or even the eight years I'd spent with Paul. But I would just ignore Hunter Williams, III and the others. They annoyed me to no end. Always had. I didn't need to spend time with them because I wasn't with Sanders anymore. I guess there was a silver lining in things, after all.

"Mackenzie?"

I looked at Nessa and shook my head. "I'm fine. Or as fine as I can be. I can't change what happened. I can only get angrier and more bitter, but I don't want to become that person. So, I'm going to focus on what I *can* change. And that is my internship and the new program. Classes and everything that has to do with me and the choices I make, and nothing having to do with the guy I thought I would spend the rest of my life with."

They all looked at me, and I thought I detected a little pity in their gazes. But there was righteous anger there, as well, so I would hold onto that. It was the least I could do.

"Well, we can be angry for you," Nessa added, and I smiled.

"I'm sure if we felt like it, we could have easily put all of my mementos of the past fifteen to twenty years of my life into a trash bin and lit it on fire. But we saw that episode of *Friends*, didn't we? Didn't they have to call the fire department?" I teased.

"But there would be hot firemen and women," Nessa put in.

"And they'd probably all be twenty years older than us," I said dryly.

"Well, maybe your rebound needs to be an older guy," Natalie put in. I did my best to blank my features.

"What do you know about rebounds?" Nessa asked, and Natalie closed her eyes.

"I read. I watch movies."

I chuckled. "I am going to ignore all of you and study. Isn't that what we should be doing? Working on our papers?"

"Yes," Elise added and set down her book. "But I don't want to. I want to pretend that I don't have to study and have things magically work out." She let out a happy little sigh. "But Dillon and I told ourselves that we would spend time with our roommates tonight and study instead of hanging out with each other."

"Exactly. If you guys hang out with each other, there will be no studying except for anatomy," Nessa teased.

"You *are* planning to be a physical therapist. It's important that you understand anatomy," Natalie said, her voice sounding sage and wise.

"So says the virgin," Nessa teased, and Natalie threw some popcorn from her bowl at her friend.

"Jerk. I don't know why my virginity is such a thing," Natalie said.

I shook my head. "It's not a thing. We just like mentioning it because you smile and joke with us about it. If we're hurting you, let us know," I urged.

Natalie smiled. "I'm a virgin because I want to be, not

because I'm waiting for the right guy. It's because I didn't have anyone I wanted to date in high school, no one I wanted enough to touch me." She shivered.

The others laughed, and I smiled. "I can see that being a problem."

"Exactly," Natalie agreed. "Maybe I'll find a guy I don't mind being with someday, but I would rather just focus on school. Maybe a relationship and sex will come."

"That's the goal of sex. Coming," Nessa added, and I groaned at the horrible joke. Suddenly, the four of us were laughing, and I felt like maybe I could do this whole roommate thing. The girls I had lived with for the two and a half years prior had all been a year older than me. I had known that they would move out one day and that I would be forced to find new roommates. But that had been part of my plan. I had been okay with the idea of having to find either girls in my year or another set who was younger like my prior roommates had done for me. But then our landlord had doubled the rent to the point that I couldn't afford it.

Bottom line: He hadn't wanted students in his place anymore. And I understood that. Especially since the guys next door, who weren't technically part of a frat since there weren't fraternities on campus, had destroyed their house. My roommates and I hadn't been that way. We had cleaned the place to within an inch of its life and left it in far better condition than we found it. But our landlord hadn't cared. He had wanted us out and adults in. I had a feeling the place would have a high turnover rate because adults didn't want to live near college students. Especially not off college row. It was silly to think that even boosters—those who gave big money to the school—would want to live in the place full-time. Any homes on that road that weren't full of students these days only seemed to be filled during holidays, during off-peak times, and if there was a football game near.

Nobody wanted to live in party central. My new home was a street over, so it wasn't as loud, but there were a lot of younger students. Ones that didn't live in the dorms or were living alone for the first time. So, it could get loud, but college row held the parties. Pacey's house, the one he shared with the guys, was on that street. I shook my head. Since when had I started thinking about it as Pacey's house?

I needed to push those thoughts from my mind and not think about him like that.

Because Pacey was not the center of my universe.

Sanders had been, and that had clearly been a mistake.

"So, what is this internship?" Natalie asked, and I looked over at my friend, shaking myself out of my thoughts.

"It's still on campus, but we get to go up to Boulder as well to work with the CU Math Department. I'll be working on proofs and giving talks and just learning what it feels like to be a professor and in the industry of my career."

"I still can't believe you're a mathematician," Nessa said, and I raised my brows at her.

"Because girls can't be good at math?" I asked dryly.

Nessa rolled her eyes. "You know I don't think that. It's more that you're hot, funny, popular, and I never knew that girls like that could be in the math program."

I rolled my eyes because I knew she was joking with me, especially if the laughter in her eyes was any indication. "Well, it's thoughts like those that make my schooling years not so much fun. The number of guys in our class is ten to one at this point. And there's only twenty of us in some of these classes," I said dryly.

"That's a little ridiculous," Elise said.

I nodded. "Some aren't as bad because there are great STEM programs for people who aren't part of the stereotype when you think of a mathematician. But it's still a boys' game, and I hate it sometimes." My professors were all men, which was odd to me since I knew there were female professors on campus in my program. But this semester, it was all men. And now we were at a point in my classes where I was mostly with those sharing my major, or some whose minors were in math, like Pacey. Gone was the time when we had more women in class because they had all moved into their majors, like physics, chemistry, and biology. There weren't many math majors out there. And I had applied mathematics, not full theory, so the scope was even narrower. I loved what I did. I loved figuring out problems and playing with numbers. Because there was an answer for all things. You could go down a path—you just needed to find it. And that's how I planned my life. To find that path.

I hated that I sometimes fell off, though.

Once again, I pushed those thoughts from my mind.

"And this program?" Nessa said. "I don't understand it."

"Me, either," Elise added. "We don't have a full thesis or anything for my senior year. You just get your credits as long as it reaches your major, and then you graduate with that degree."

I shrugged. "Not all majors are like this. And not all universities are like this one. But mine has a final senior thesis for your undergrad that leads you to your master's classes that you can take at this campus. But a lot of times, they want you to be at another campus before you go on to your doctorate. It's a whole long, complicated mess. And that means I'll be writing thesis after thesis until I decide to retire." I shrugged. "I don't mind it. It's math. It makes sense."

"To you," Nessa said dryly.

"To me," I said with a smile. "But this is the semester where everything starts to settle into place for your senior year. And then, after that, you're an adult, not just playing adult, like I feel most of us are doing in college."

"Nothing you have ever said has been so true," Nessa said with a laugh.

"Are you going to have time for any extracurriculars?" Natalie asked.

I frowned, shaking my head. "I'm taking an extra three-credit-hours class. I wasn't planning to this semester, but they moved it from the fall to the spring. I needed to add it so I wouldn't miss out and have to take another year." I sighed. "I can't even get the part-time job I wanted to apply for so I'd have some extra spending money."

"But your parents are helping you out?" Nessa asked.

I cringed. "Yes, and no. They saved for college and are paying for every other semester. My loans pay for the rest. I had to get an additional loan for spending money, but that's fine," I added as the girls sighed. "I'm not insane when it comes to spending and rent, and everything will be paid for. It's just not something I planned on, which is the theme of this semester."

"You can't plan everything, Mackenzie, but you can do your best," Elise said, then sighed. "I guess the only fun you'll have is with us and when we hang out with the guys."

I pressed my lips together and nodded. "Are we hanging out with the guys a lot?"

"Of course, we are," Nessa said. "They're our friends. And you-know-who doesn't live there anymore, so it'll be easier for you, right?"

I sighed. "Maybe." I let out a breath, knowing that I needed to talk this big thing out, even if it wasn't easy.

"I also have an idea that might be weird."

"How weird?" Nessa asked.

"One second," Elise said and looked down at her phone. "It's Dillon. He said we'd talk later. Is this okay? I can call him back."

I looked at the eager faces of my friends and smiled. "We can talk about it later."

Or never.

How could I bring up the fact that our friend—Nessa's best friend now—had offered to be my rebound?

I didn't even know what I wanted out of that.

No, it'd be better to keep it to myself.

At least until I figured out what I wanted.

If that time ever came.

Four

Pacey

"How have you never had chicken parm before?" Tanner asked. I shrugged, looking down at the very delicious-looking, cheesy and saucy concoction that my roommate had prepared.

"I don't know. I've seen it on the tele, but I don't think my mother likes tomatoes all that much. It wasn't a thing we ate."

Tanner shook his head and began plating our meals. "You guys are missing out."

"It looks it." I took the plate from him and passed it down the line to Miles and Dillon.

"I am a little spoiled with you and Dillon constantly making us food." Miles groaned.

I grinned. "I know, right? We don't even need to cook. We're just in charge of dishes all the time."

"Because the two of you aren't allowed to cook unless it's chopping cheese into cubes and putting crackers on a plate."

"Thank God charcuterie is in right now," I said dryly, and Miles snorted. "You can at least do that. Mine looks like a Lunchable that's been tipped over."

"That is true," I said solemnly, and Miles flipped me off.

We made our way into the kitchenette rather than the formal dining room. The other area was a little too big for the four of us, but I was starving, so I didn't care where we ate. We sat down and dug in, and I took my first bite. Spices and tomato and cheese burst on my tongue, and I groaned aloud.

"Dear God, where have you been all my life?" I said after I swallowed, and Tanner grinned.

"I told you you'd like it."

Dillon shook his head. "And I didn't dispute the fact that he would. You and I are going to have to find out what other things he's missed over the years."

"You act as if I haven't lived in America for the past decade. Just because my mother doesn't like tomatoes or pasta doesn't mean that I have hidden from all food that's not UK-involved."

"You say that, and yet, in my head, you've only eaten fish and chips," Dillon said and winked.

"Once you guys can make me decent fish and chips, we will talk. But don't you dare bring me tartar sauce."

"What's wrong with tartar sauce?" Miles asked and then took a big bite of his pasta.

"We use malt vinegar, thank you very much."

"I remember going to Epcot once," Tanner put in, his voice low. "Mom asked for tartar sauce when we were in the England part, and they gave her such a look of shock for even asking that she went away and ate them without anything."

I shook my head. "I thought Disney World was supposed to have the happiest people on Earth."

"Maybe, but our trip ended with my mother annoyed that she couldn't get what she wanted with the fish and chips."

"Well, if you ever head over to actual England and not just the one in Orlando, Florida, I'll show you around."

Tanner snorted. "I don't see that happening, buddy."

I raised a brow. "You don't want to spend time with me, then?" I asked, teasing.

"No, I don't see myself able to afford a trip to England."

I shrugged. "We can make it happen."

"You're not paying for me to go to England." Tanner practically growled the words, and I nodded.

"Fine. Maybe I can stuff you in my luggage."

"You could try," Tanner said and then snorted. "Man, I'm a good cook."

Tanner never really complimented himself or said anything about himself at all. The fact that we had not only gotten a childhood story and him mentioning some good things about his food out of him meant that Tanner was in a good mood tonight.

"Anyway, how are your classes going?" Dillon asked as we kept eating.

Miles shrugged. "They're okay, I think. I don't know

how it's going to be until the first exam. That's how it is for me, anyway."

Tanner nodded. "Sometimes, it's the same for me. My goal is not to stay up late studying before the exam, though. And to keep up on my paperwork." He snorted. "Let's see if it happens."

"I am taking two more labs than I thought I would, and they're only one credit. But having consistent, four to five-hour times sitting in a classroom, working with my hands, I may need to start drinking more," I said dryly.

"I never understood that about science labs. They take more time than the course itself and yet are only one credit. It's ridiculous."

"I have a feeling it's because the people who assign those credit hours don't understand what those labs are needed for. And the people who provide the material for it know, and might feel bad about the one measly credit hour, but they also know that you can't move on to the next semester until you know certain things. Especially since we're all entering the last semester of our junior year. We need to know these things so we can go off to grad school or start our careers. We can't just hope we're going to understand what we're doing without actually learning anything."

"You're going to end up a professor, aren't you?" Tanner drawled.

I shrugged. "I'm going to grad school. I think I want to go into industry, mostly because I like keeping a roof over my head and am accustomed to certain aspects of my monetary life."

Dillon snorted. "Whatever you say."

"I think I'll know more once I'm in grad school. I have

half a mind to go one way, yet the other part of me wants to work with my hands rather than in a classroom. I don't know yet, and that bothers me."

Tanner nodded. "We're all at that point where we have to decide what we're going to do with the rest of our lives. It's not at all frightening," he drawled.

"Not at all," I agreed.

My phone buzzed, and I pulled it out of my pocket, wondering if it was my parents. They hadn't contacted me since they told me about the divorce a week ago, but at a glance, I saw it wasn't them. A small smile played over my face at the name on the readout.

"Who is it? Sasha?" Dillon asked.

"Sasha is sadly still with her boyfriend. We're just friends."

"Nessa, then," Miles said decidedly. "Although I still don't know why you don't just date her," he grumbled.

I gave the other man a look and shook my head. "Nessa and I are only friends. It's what we both want."

Miles rolled his eyes, but I ignored him. Instead, I started typing.

Me: *I'm glad you're thinking about me.*

Mackenzie: *I asked what you were doing, not that I was thinking about you. Why are you so weird?*

I smiled again, and Tanner cleared his throat.

"Who is it?"

"I'll tell you in a moment."

Mostly because I had to, or they wouldn't leave me alone about it. And a conundrum would approach if I didn't explain.

Mackenzie: *I've thought about it, and I suppose we can* *try dinner. Just to see. Mostly because I need to get out of the house and pretend that I'm not focusing on school while pretending that people aren't giving me pitying looks about Paul.*

I smiled again.

Me: *I love that you call him Paul.*

Mackenzie: *He was Paul to me before he was Sanders. It's not a derogatory term like you use.*

Me: *That's not what I hear. It's all derogatory, all the time.*

Mackenzie: *So, what did you have in mind to get through this rebound?*

Thoughts of exactly what we could do filled my mind, but I pushed them away. Mackenzie was my friend. I wouldn't be her exact rebound. I would be who she needed me to be, even if she didn't realize it.

Me: *I'll pick you up tomorrow night, and we'll go to dinner. Wear something nice, but not too fancy. We are on a budget.*

Mackenzie: *You know I need to know where. I like plans.*

Me: *I'm going to teach you the joy of spontaneity.*

Mackenzie: *This isn't going to work out. You obviously don't know me that well.*

I laughed, aware that the three guys were still staring at me.

Me: *Fine, I was thinking of going to Clancy's. It's a nice little bistro made for college students on dates. It's not too expensive. You can wear a soft dress. I will be my perfect British self and even wrap my scarf around your shoulders if it gets too cold out. It is a Denver winter.*

Mackenzie: *How charming. Will I meet you there?*

I sighed, and Dillon leaned forward. I held up a hand and then continued to type.

Me: *I will pick you up, as I said. I'll see you tomorrow at six.*

Mackenzie: *Okay, then. I hope I'm not making a mistake.*

I hoped we weren't either.

Me: *You aren't. You just need to get out, as you said. And I'll be your perfect rebound.*

Mackenzie: *Whatever that is.*

I set down the phone and looked up to see the three guys focused on me, bemused expressions on their faces.

Miles narrowed his eyes. "Who the hell was that? You were smiling and doing that flirting thing with your face."

I frowned. "Flirting thing with my face?"

Tanner snorted. "You know, when you raise a brow and pucker your lips and look like you're a teenage vampire."

That made me laugh. "A teenage vampire?"

"Yes, maybe a Salvatore or a Cullen," Tanner drawled.

"You sure do know a lot about teenage vampires," Dillon drawled, and I grinned.

"What he said," I added.

"Really, who is it? Do we know her?" Dillon asked, and I cleared my throat. No time like the present to just peel off that Band-Aid.

"It's Mackenzie."

All three of them stared at me and blinked.

"As in Sanders' Mackenzie?" Miles asked.

I scowled. "As in Mackenzie's Mackenzie. She is no longer with that asshole, thank you very much."

Miles held up both hands. "I'm sorry. It's just...she was

with Sanders forever. They're always going to be connected in some way."

"No, they're not. And that is what we are trying to accomplish. To sever that tie, that connection. That way, when someone utters the name *Mackenzie*, nobody even thinks of Sanders."

The guys just looked at me.

"Isn't there a code? You know, not poaching on another guy's girl?" Dillon asked slowly, his voice low. "Not that I'm going to call you a poacher, but Sanders *was* our roommate. None of us might like the guy all that much anymore, but it's still a thing, isn't it?"

"I have to agree with Dillon," Tanner added.

I shook my head. "There's no code. Sanders isn't our friend any longer. And I'm not poaching. I'm her rebound," I said, and they just blinked at me.

"Really? You're just labeling yourself like that?" Dillon asked incredulously.

I shook my head. "She said that she needed a rebound, that she needed someone people would think about and mutter under their breath about so they knew she was over Sanders and fine. And I offered to be that person."

"Magnanimously," Tanner drawled.

"I'm exactly who she needs," I added.

"So, you like her?" Miles asked, blinking. "I thought you were with Nessa."

"Hell, so did I," Dillon muttered.

"They're not wrong," Tanner added.

I shook my head and rolled my shoulders back. "Nessa and I are friends, something you all know. Nessa even went out on a date with another guy. We are *just* friends.

Mackenzie and I will also be friends. But she wants to get out and have fun and not have the world think that she's pining away for some guy who never deserved her in the first place. So, I'm her friend."

"And you're not going to want to sleep with her?" Tanner asked, a growl in his voice.

I sighed. "It doesn't matter what I want. It matters what Mackenzie wants. And she wants to pretend that she's fine. Go out and act as if nothing has happened. And I will be that person for her. I will be her friend. There's no code because, number one, we hate Sanders, and he's not our friend or roommate anymore. And I'm not going to change the dynamic of our relationship. Mackenzie is our friend. I just want to make sure she understands that."

"That's a very convoluted way of showing that you're a good guy," Dillon said after a moment of silence.

I shrugged. "I'm not always a good guy, but I like Mackenzie. She's a good person. She's funny, and she's brilliant. And Sanders is still standing in her way, even if it's just his ghost."

"And you plan to push that ghost away?" Tanner asked, his voice low.

I shrugged again. "I'm going to let Mackenzie do that for herself. But if she needs someone to stand by her side, I'll do that. Because I'm her friend."

The guys gave me looks but then thankfully changed the subject, letting my lies stand.

Because I *was* Mackenzie's friend. I didn't want anything more than what I had offered. I didn't have time for that. And, honestly, my life was far more complicated than most believed. I didn't need to add things to my day.

I wanted to be Mackenzie's friend. Just like she was mine.

And, honestly, if I made Sanders growl and get annoyed in the process, I counted that as a win.

But for now, Mackenzie would come first.

For once.

FIVE

Mackenzie

I HAD BEEN THIRTEEN WHEN I WENT ON MY FIRST real date. Thirteen years old. That'd happened seven years ago. Now, I was going on my second first date, and I had no idea what to wear.

"You look wonderful," Natalie said from the doorway. I looked over at her and gave her a dubious smile.

"I look like I have no idea what I'm doing."

I decided not to go with a dress, mostly because it was cooler outside. Though it didn't help that as soon as Pacey had mentioned a dress, I had gotten this weird fluttery sensation in my stomach. Tonight wasn't about falling or being with someone I cared about beyond friendship. It was about moving on. I didn't know what else it *could* be and stay sane.

I had decided to go with my black jumpsuit, which could be casual or fancy depending on the shoes and jewelry and bag I wore with it. I was also going with a cute wrap thing over it since I didn't want my arms bare. All in all, I thought it looked okay, but I hoped it was enough. And not too much, all at the same time.

Why was I doing this again?

"So, you and Pacey...?" Natalie began again, and I shook my head.

"We're just friends."

"Okay, so this is just a friend date?"

I nodded. "Yes, we're going out to dinner so I can get used to the whole leaving the house thing. It's not, you know, anything serious." I studied my reflection in the mirror and ignored the line between my brows that told me I wasn't even sure *I* believed my words.

She nodded and smiled softly. "Pacey's a good guy. And I like that he's doing this so your *next* first date is something nice, rather than something you have to be super nervous for."

I smiled, inwardly cringing at the idea of *another* first date even if it was imaginary and in the future. "Exactly. However, the concept seems weird and out there. That's why I didn't tell the other girls. It's not like I'm keeping it a secret, though. If they see me out and about, I'll talk to them about it. But we don't talk about everybody we go on dates with. Not that I've ever been on a date with anybody. It's only ever been Sanders. Though because I don't want it to only ever *be* Sanders, this is it. My rebound. One I can still be friends with after, no matter what happens."

Natalie gave me a weird look but nodded. "Sounds like

a plan. But you're going to have to tell Nessa and Elise. You're all friends. Including Pacey. They're going to figure it out. "

I pressed my lips together, and nerves wrapped around my body like a vise. "Yes, but I don't want it to be a big deal."

"It might be a big deal," she whispered.

I shook my head. "It won't. This is just something light and easy to start the semester off right."

I knew I was lying to myself at this point, but that would have to be acceptable. I could continue doing so if needed.

"Is he meeting you there?"

"No, he's picking me up here."

Natalie's brows rose. "I guess there won't be any hiding."

I cringed. "That's not what I was doing. I just didn't know how to bring it up. I'm not hiding."

"Okay. I believe you. I really do."

"Then why do I feel like I keep doing things wrong?"

"Because none of this was part of your master plan," she said softly.

"And now why do I feel like a dork for even having a master plan?"

"You're not a dork. You're allowed to have goals. I love you," she whispered, and I shook my head.

"I love you, too, even though I *feel* like a complete dork."

The doorbell rang, and my eyes widened.

"I'll go open the door for him. Nessa is out on a date, although I don't think it's going to work out with the guy."

I frowned. "Is it George?"

"No, I think it's Jeff. I don't know. But this is their

second date. I really don't know. She doesn't seem into it. Elise is with Dillon, so that's nice."

"Yes, they're really into it, unlike Nessa."

My stomach clenched as Natalie left to let Pacey in. I picked up my bag, rechecked my makeup, and then grabbed my large coat to go over my wrap and jumpsuit. This would have to do. Even though I had a feeling that I might throw up or something later. This was way too stressful.

I walked into the living room and saw Pacey standing there, talking to Natalie. He wore a peacoat over gray slacks and a gray shirt, and had brushed his hair back. Still, that one blond piece kept falling over his forehead. I always wanted to reach out and push it back, but that wasn't my place. We were just friends. It wouldn't be my place tonight, either. Unless it was? What exactly did a rebound entail? What did he think would happen tonight? What did I expect?

I put my hand over my stomach and let out a breath.

I didn't expect anything. This was as free and easy as I could be without a plan.

And I was drowning.

Natalie cleared her throat as I walked into the room. Pacey pulled his gaze from mine, and it was only then that I realized he had been staring at me just like I had been staring at him.

This isn't awkward at all.

"Well, I'm going back to my room. Alone. Since I'm the only one without a date. However, I'm used to this. And I'm going to stop talking. Bye." Natalie gave a little wave and practically ran towards her room. The door closed behind her, and I stood a few feet away from Pacey, wondering if I was making a mistake. I was probably making a huge mistake.

Pacey cleared his throat. "You look wonderful," he said.

I bit my lip. "Maybe. I don't know." That wasn't really what I was supposed to say. "You look wonderful, too. Or nice. I should really have notecards or something."

Pacey's lips twitched, and he held out his hand. "Are you ready?"

"Maybe?" I asked, then slid my hand into his.

"I guess I'm going to have to take that as an affirmative." He squeezed my hand and led me outside. I quickly locked the door behind me to keep Natalie safe and then made my way down the front steps towards Pacey's car.

"How did you secure a spot right in front of the house?"

Pacey shrugged. "Magic, I imagine."

"Huh, I can never do that. Luckily, we have spaces behind the house, but it's a tight fit with four cars."

"Dillon occasionally parks on the street near our home," Pacey said but frowned. I knew he remembered the last time Dillon had parked on the street, but we both brushed over that topic. We didn't need to talk about things that hurt. Not tonight. At least, I hoped so.

"Well, you won the lottery on parking spots, so we'll call it that."

He opened the door for me, and I slid inside his black car and inhaled the scent of leather. He got it on the other side, and I raised a brow. "I didn't know you had such a fancy car."

"I bet you don't know a lot of things about me, Mackenzie. But I guess that's what tonight's for."

I swallowed hard, nerves and something else twisting inside me. "I guess so."

He studied my face, smiled, and then pulled out of the parking spot. We could have walked the few blocks to the restaurant, but it was cold, and I wore heels. I was glad he had driven. It gave me a moment to think where we talked about school and classes and nothing substantial.

Was this what dating was? Talking about common interests and random things that might not matter in the end? What did Sanders and I ever talk about? Our futures and what was going on, but clearly not all of it. I hadn't talked about my internship with him. We talked about what would happen once we left school, but nothing else. Maybe I was just thinking too hard about it.

Soon, I found myself sitting across from Pacey in the restaurant, candlelight flickering between us and music playing overhead. The waitress had poured us both water as neither of us had ordered soda or juice. Not being twenty-one yet sort of ruined things. But I had a birthday coming up, and Pacey should have, too, since he was in the same year as I was.

"What were you thinking about that made you frown?" Pacey asked as I looked up at him.

"What?"

"You were frowning. I was giving you a lovely anecdote about chicken parm, and Tanner's amazing skills in the kitchen and my lack, and you weren't even listening."

"Chicken parm?" I asked.

Pacey sighed and tapped the menu absently. "Where is your head right now? Because it's not here."

I blushed and ducked my head. "Sorry. I was just

thinking about what you're supposed to do on a date. I've only dated one person. I'm not really good at this." I blushed. "Not that this is a date. Or that it isn't. I really don't know. We probably should have made more sense of it. I'm really sorry, and I'm talking really fast. I should stop saying 'really' because it makes me sound like I'm fourteen."

Pacey shook his head and smiled at the waitress as she came by. She only had eyes for him, and I didn't blame her. He was magnetic, beautiful, and everybody around him always gravitated towards him.

I always had. He had been a friend. He was *still* a friend. Whatever tonight was wouldn't go anywhere. I just had to keep reminding myself of that.

"Are you ready to order, Mackenzie?" Pacey asked. I looked up in time to see him staring at me. Still, the waitress only had eyes for him.

I cleared my throat. "The soup and salad."

He shook his head. "You can have a real dinner."

"I like their soup. And their salad's refreshing. I've had the chicken here before, but I want the soup tonight."

Pacey's eyes brightened, and he nodded. "I'll have the chicken. But I might have to steal a sip of that soup."

"Oh, I can give you some soup if you'd like. Just a small taste," the waitress said, and I barely resisted the urge to roll my eyes.

Pacey cleared his throat. "I'm sure my date and I will be fine. Thank you, Cathy."

She fluttered her hands, took the menus away, and left.

"Do women always do that around you?"

He shrugged. "Some do. But I'm sure they do the same with you."

I shook my head. "I think the world always knew I was with Sanders. I've been off-limits."

"No man ever flirted with you?"

I frowned. "Maybe? I'm not good at figuring it out."

"Let me just lay it out here. Tonight, whatever I say to you, I'm flirting with you."

I blushed and took a sip of my water. "Oh."

"Yes, oh. Now, should we discuss our physics class? Or maybe our math class?"

"I'm only in one physics class this semester. And you're in it."

Pacey nodded. "I was sitting in the back while you were up front. I got in late because I met with my advisor. Sadly, I couldn't get the seat I wanted. Having the class only on Fridays is a bit different for me."

I nodded. "Oh, I'm glad you're in it. I don't know a lot of people there. I kept having to put off the class because it interfered with my labs. Now, I feel like I'm the only junior in there."

"There are at least two of us."

"Why didn't you take it before? It's part of your major."

"I took the second and third classes that come in a row after it. But thanks to a scheduling snafu, I couldn't get in the first year. So, I'm taking it now, even though I already have the material after it. But I can't test out."

"That's horrible," I said.

"It'll hopefully be an A for me, but I'll sit next to you if you'd like. We can study together."

"Even if this rebound misses?" I teased nervously.

He reached out and grabbed my hand. "No matter what happens, we're friends, Mackenzie. Promise me."

My heart twisted just a little, a slow tangle of nerves that didn't tell me exactly what they meant. "I was going to ask you to pledge that..."

He squeezed my hand again. "Good. Now, promise me."

"I promise. No matter what."

"Good," he repeated. "Now, as for our math class, I think I'm in two of them with you. Am I correct?"

I nodded. "Yes, though a gaggle of girls surrounded you, so I didn't sit next to you."

Pacey rolled his eyes. "We'll sit together next time. You're going to have so much Pacey in your life, you'll get annoyed and sick of me."

"I don't think I could get sick of you, Pacey. You're a nice guy."

He winced. "That's the worst thing you can say to a man on a date. Nice?"

"I need nice in my life, Pacey. Especially a nice friend."

"I see I've been put in my place," he said and shook his head. "Anyway, what do you think of Dr. Michaels?"

I sighed. "I hate him." I paused, my eyes going wide. "I can't believe I just said that."

"He's an asshole. He's a misogynistic asshole who only likes people like him. But he's our professor."

"He is," I said sadly. "And I need him to be my advisor for the last two semesters here. I'm already on track for his internship. The papers just need to be signed."

His eyes widened, and he beamed. "That's a hard internship to get into. Congratulations."

I smiled softly. "I've worked my ass off. I'm just grateful that it worked out."

"Me, too. I'm working for another professor. Dr. Jackson."

My eyes went wide. "Oh, I love her. I had her down as my backup, even though you can't call her a backup because she's brilliant. But the thesis I want to do is more geared towards Dr. Michaels' specialties. And so, here we are."

"It makes sense," Pacey said. "We're going to be busy the next year and a half or so."

"And then grad school after. And then careers, and futures, and whatever personal lives we can forge around it. It's going to be a lot."

"I take it you have your plans set out?"

I blushed. "Yes, at least professionally. My personal life plan is sort of out the window now."

"And yet, here you are, flying and soaring in new directions."

"And hopefully not drowning," I muttered as our dinners arrived. I ignored the way our waitress flirted with Pacey again.

I didn't know why it annoyed me so much. Pacey wasn't my boyfriend, but it bothered me nonetheless. "She knows I'm on a date with you. You've called me your date."

"She's persistent." He held up a piece of paper with a phone number on it. "Should we call her later?"

I rolled my eyes. "You're welcome to, but she's not part of my rebound."

"Good to know," Pacey said. "Now, are you going to feed me?"

"Not even a little. But you're welcome to have a bite."

"A single bite? Oh, no, Mackenzie. I think I could use more. Just a single morsel."

I ignored the flirting and the way it made me feel, all tight and oddly needy. Instead, we ate and laughed, and he was his perfectly British and flirty self.

By the time we finished dinner, I was full, happy, and wondering if this was how dates were supposed to be. There was no stress. Only fun. And yet, I was still nervous. Because of what would come next. What came after the first date? What was supposed to?

What did I want?

Pacey pulled up in front of the house, this time taking a spot behind the one he had before, but still in a prime position. "What kind of sorcery do you possess?" I asked, shaking my head.

Pacey grinned and raised a brow. I swallowed hard. "Wouldn't you like to know?"

"Oh," I breathed. "Well..." I began and then trailed off.

Pacey shook his head. "Let me walk you to the door."

Disappointment surged, and yet I felt relief. I nodded. "Okay. That works."

He smiled again. "It's getting colder. I do believe snow is on the way. So, let's get you inside where you'll be warm."

Was I supposed to invite him in? What was I supposed to do? Everything had just come naturally with Sanders, so naturally, it had imploded.

What was I supposed to think now?

Why was this so hard?

And why did I have to keep comparing him to Sanders? Because Pacey wasn't Paul. I didn't want him to be. I didn't want *anyone* to be. I needed to push those thoughts and memories away and never think about them again. But they were so ingrained in my past, present, and future, that I didn't know how I was supposed to do anything.

Pacey opened the door while I had been wool-gathering, and I looked up at him, then swallowed hard once again. He held out his hand and smiled. Such a sweet expression that went right to his eyes and did wicked things to his face. I ignored the twist low in my belly and slid my hand into his as I got out of the car. I closed the door behind me, and he tangled his fingers with mine and held my hand as he kept me steady and we walked up the stairs.

I was holding hands with Pacey Ziglar.

I had gone on a date with Pacey Ziglar.

As I stood on the front step and looked up at him, I didn't know what else I might do with Pacey Ziglar.

He tilted his head and pushed my hair away from my face. "Did you have a good time tonight, Mackenzie?"

I licked my lips, and his gaze went straight to them. "I did. I am."

He smiled then, and I lifted my chin and opened my mouth a bit, not knowing what I should say or do.

Pacey kept his gaze on mine as if asking for permission. I nodded ever so slightly, and he lowered his lips to mine, just a gentle brush, a sweet caress, He kissed me, a quick kiss, somewhat more pressure than a peck but no full sensation. When he pulled away, I realized that he was only the second boy I'd ever kissed.

The second one I would ever kiss.

I tried to say something, attempted to say thank you or tell him to have a good night, but nothing came out. Instead, I hiccuped, and the tears fell. All I could do was look at him, mortified.

Pacey gave me a small smile and pushed my hair back from my face again.

"It's okay, Mackenzie. It's about time you did this."

I looked at him, confused, even as the tears fell harder. "You expected me to cry after you kissed me?"

"I expected you to feel something. To cry, to do anything...long before this. You are so strong, Mackenzie. You don't have to hide it anymore."

"So this was just a ruse? To make me cry?" I asked through sobs. He clicked his tongue, a move quite odd for a boy his age, but then pulled me close. I stiffened in his hold, my head resting on his chest, but slowly wrapped my arms around his waist and let myself weep. I cried for the girl I had been, for the one I would never be again.

And for the future that had broken beneath my feet.

I cried in the arms of the boy who held me, who made me smile, made me laugh. Made me feel. And I'd never been more confused in my life.

Six

Pacey

I COUGHED INTO MY HAND, ANNOYED WITH MYSELF. I walked into my bathroom, washed my hands, cleaned my face, and sucked nasal spray up my nose. I added eyedrops and took another antibiotic.

I was exhausted, but that's what happened when you got a sinus infection out of the blue. I was used to infections by now, but I didn't usually get them during the first month of school. However, it had been a hard winter, after a summer full of fires and smoke, so I shouldn't be surprised that my sinuses were acting up now. Thankfully, I seemed to be on the mend, but I was still a little tired. I was also a bit short of breath, though I knew that came from the postnasal drip lovingly coursing down my throat and entering my lungs, but hopefully, I wouldn't need to be hospitalized again.

When I was younger, I had always likened myself to the kid from *My Girl*. Only instead of bees, it was anything and everything else. My mother had always sobbed when we watched that movie, and I didn't know why she continued watching it, even now. I was pretty sure the damn thing was older than I was.

I saw myself in that kid, though. The first kiss and then finding a ring for a girl just because they were your best friend.

And then dying because bees sucked, and life was cruel.

I pushed those odd thoughts away and shook my head. I just needed to get through today. I rewashed my hands, added some hand sanitizer just in case, and winged my way downstairs. I had a study date with Nessa. Although we weren't in the same classes this semester, we still wanted to study together. She always made me think, and I enjoyed her company. We used to be the three musketeers with Corinne around, and I hated that she was no longer with us.

I didn't know what I was supposed to do with her gone. Though I had faced my mortality at a young age, I wasn't sure I'd known what it meant for others to die around me.

I frowned, taking the final steps as the doorbell rang.

"Nessa?" Miles asked from the his study area. He and Tanner shared the library, while Dillon and I shared the office. Sanders had occupied the desk in the back alcove area that worked for him. Now, it was the catch-all for all of our extra books and notebooks. We were less than a month into school and were already getting messy. I'd have to work on cleaning things up. It just went to remind me that I had a feeling that it wasn't Sanders who had kept us clean last semester but rather his girlfriend.

Mackenzie. The girl that I had made cry.

I pushed those thoughts from my head once again. I hadn't meant to make her cry. But I was glad that she'd finally felt something. Wasn't I?

"She's here to study," I said, finally answering Miles.

He gave me a hard look. "So... Nessa *and* Mackenzie?"

I narrowed my eyes at my friend and roommate, trying to understand what his problem could be. "Do you have a problem with that?"

"No, not really. I like them both. Just be careful."

I frowned at Miles. "Do you have a prior claim I'm not aware of?" I asked, honestly interested.

"No claim," Miles said again. "I promise. Just don't hurt them, okay?"

I frowned, blinking. "I need to get Nessa so I don't leave her out in the cold, but we're going to talk more about this. I'm not going to hurt them. I'm their friend."

"Do they know that?" he asked and then walked back into the library, closing the door softly behind him.

The doorbell rang again. My phone buzzed, and I cursed, making my way to the front door. Miles and I needed to talk. I wasn't the asshole he thought I was, and I wanted to make sure he understood that. Because I sure as hell didn't want to hurt my friends. I had to make sure they understood that.

I opened the door quickly, and Nessa pushed her way in, her teeth chattering. "Leave me hanging next time, why don't you?" she chided, and I shook my head. "I am so sorry, darling. Miles waylaid me, but I'm here now."

"Well, thank you. It is cold out there. Colder than a witch's tit."

I started. "I don't think I've ever heard you utter that phrase."

She winced, her already reddened cheeks turning redder. "It's something my dad used to say, and I wanted to try it out. I don't think it's me."

"Not really. Especially since I don't think you've ever said the word *tit* in front of me before."

She flushed more and ducked her head. "Oh, well, I guess I didn't think about that. Anyway..." she said, muttering to herself.

I shook my head and took her coat. "Do you want to study in the living room, my room, or at my desk? Dillon is at class. I think he's bringing Elise home later."

"I guess down here's fine. That way other people can study with us if they want. I guess. Is Mackenzie joining us?" she asked quickly, and I frowned, leading her towards the living room.

"Not that I know of. Though we are going to try a study session since we're in two classes together and working towards a similar thesis."

She nodded as she set her books down, rocking from foot to foot. Why was she so nervous? "Oh, so you guys have a lot in common?"

"I guess so. I like her. I hate what that asshole did to her."

Nessa scowled. "That asshole never deserved her. She deserves the world. She's so sweet and amazing, though I guess you already know that, don't you?"

"What aren't you saying?" I asked, honestly curious.

She shrugged as she sat down and took her books out of her bag. "She mentioned that she went out to dinner with you but didn't say how it went. I was asleep when you guys got home."

I sighed, wondering what I was missing. "I took Mackenzie out to dinner because she said she wanted to get out into the world and not have everybody think of her as the poor girl who Sanders cheated on. But she and I were and *are* just friends."

At least that's what I told myself. Mackenzie wasn't ready for anything, and God knew I didn't have time for it. It didn't matter that I kept thinking about her, or that she made me smile and laugh. And we *did* have things in common. Mackenzie wasn't for me, though. And I sure as hell wasn't for her.

And nothing would change that.

"Oh," Nessa smiled. "Shit. I didn't even think about that. We met Mackenzie first before realizing she was with Sanders. I guess it turned into a whole thing. I don't see her and think of what Sanders did. I see a girl I like and admire."

"So do I," I said. "As my friend," I added.

Nessa smiled again. "I'm glad she has friends like you."

"Like you're my friend?"

Nessa smiled even brighter. "Exactly. We can all use someone. You know?"

"I know. Now that we have that out of the way, what are we studying tonight? Because I have proofs to work on. I may jump from something high if I have to work on them for too long."

She snorted. "I'm glad I don't have to work on what you do."

"You are the English major," I said softly. "While I like reading, I don't see myself ever writing a book."

"Hey, someone needs to write those math textbooks."

"And I could get the royalties," I said. "However, don't get Dillon started on the textbook racket. He never shuts up about it."

"You say that, but at least you all have feasible plans. I'm going to end up working at a Pizza Hut," she grumbled.

"Haven't Pizza Huts closed?" I asked, only marginally joking.

Nessa dramatically threw her head back and sighed. "I knew it. This is the end. I have no hope."

I shook my head, laughing. "If that's what you say. But I've heard you mention that you want to change your major. Is that the truth?"

She shrugged and looked down at her hands. "I don't know. Maybe I could have a future doing something that's in STEM, or business like Dillon. Something tangible."

I reached out and gripped her hand, squeezing it. She froze and looked up at me. "Without the arts, we would be nothing. Without books, without film, without something for us to relax with and enjoy and embrace, there is no reason. When we are sick or unable to move around or just want to relax, what do we do? We pick up a book. We put on our favorite show. That's art. And we need artists to create. If you want to go down your track of being an author, do so. And thrive. If you want to continue on your path to becoming an English professor, do it. You love that arena. You would be an amazing teacher. You could teach others to love it beyond getting their first course out of the way. Do it."

I leaned back into the couch, a little embarrassed to have gone on as I had. Nessa blinked at me, tears filling her eyes.

"Shit, don't cry."

"Don't curse at me," Nessa said, the tears freely falling now. She reached into her bag for tissues and wiped at her face. "That's the most beautiful, heartwarming, and inspiring thing anyone's ever said to me. And I think I hate you and love you all at the same time." She blinked suddenly, closing her mouth at her last words. I smiled, taking them at face value. We were friends. I loved her, too.

"Are you guys going to continue crying in here, or are we allowed to come in and actually study?" Tanner drawled as he came in and threw himself into the armchair. "I have a paper I have to write, and I'm contemplating paying someone to do it."

I looked over at my roommate, grateful for the reprieve. "I never once figured you as the type to pay someone."

"If I have to, I will," Tanner muttered, then looked between us and pulled out his laptop. "Don't mind me. Continue your heart-to-heart. I'm going to study and pretend I enjoy school."

Nessa settled back into the couch. "You like school. I've heard you mention it."

Tanner narrowed his eyes at her before lowering his gaze and glaring at his books. At least he wasn't glaring at us.

We went back to studying, none of us talking to each other as we did. We were each in different classes. Oddly enough, however, Mackenzie was the only one I had courses with this semester. We were all headed towards various majors, though my minor was the same as Mackenzie's primary area of study.

"Are we planning another party in a couple of weeks?" Tanner asked out of the blue, and I pulled myself from my work. I had to solve this equation, and I was already on page six of my graph paper. I had a feeling I had made a mistake around page two.

"Party?" I asked.

"Yes, party. Everyone else seems to be on the schedule already, and one of the guys down the way asked if we were going to do one this semester. He was kind of bitchy about it, so I assumed he thought we weren't going to join in and try to beat them or some shit."

I looked at my roommate and rolled my eyes at Nessa. "So, we're in competition with the brutes at the other end of the street now?"

Tanner sighed. "*They* think so."

"Brutes?" Nessa asked.

"They're the guys who would be on a football team if we actually had one."

"We have a hockey team. One that does pretty damn well, too," Nessa argued.

I raised a brow. "Thinking about catching a hockey player's interests, are you?" I asked.

She ducked her head. "I was talking about the sports, not the size of their thighs."

Tanner threw his head back and laughed. "Well, that's an image I'm never going to get out of my head. However, I dated a hockey player once. Nessa has it right about their size."

He held out his fist, and Nessa grinned and bumped his with hers.

"I'm pretty sure what you and that hockey player did had nothing to do with dating," I drawled.

"Maybe," Tanner said, drawing out his words. "Anyway,

the guys in the house aren't hockey players. I don't think they've ever actually been on ice other than driving poorly on it."

"And they want you to throw a party?" Nessa asked.

"So they can drink our beer, take our women, and pretend they know what the fuck they're doing."

"Your women?" Nessa kept going, and I laughed.

"Yes, because we've laid claim to them all."

"Sure, you have. I totally believe you."

"As for the party, I don't know. Sanders usually handled most of that for us."

"Asshole," Tanner mumbled.

"Sanders? I thought it was you," Nessa said, frowning.

"Sanders picked the dates because he pushed us to have them. He also usually got the beer because of his brother."

"I'm twenty-one now. I can handle it," Tanner said.

I nodded. "As is Miles. And the rest of us will be soon. However, it was usually Mackenzie and I who did most of the planning."

"Well, if you need help, I'm here. The girls and I enjoy coming to the parties, but we don't want to have one at our house." She winced. "No offense."

"None taken. I don't really like people in here either, but thankfully we have locks on the doors," Tanner added.

"Thankfully," I agreed. "Maybe in a couple of weeks?" I looked down at the social calendar they'd put up on the site and frowned.

"There's a calendar?" Nessa asked and pulled out her phone. "Why am I so behind the times?"

"It's a stupid thing in the school app for college row houses. It's pretty much so they can decide who's footing the bill next and not miss out on anything," I said, and Nessa nodded.

"Good, you know I hate it when I'm not in the know."

"So we hear," Tanner said, shaking his head. "Okay, I need to go work on a few things in my room, and then I have a date tonight."

"Tonight?" I blinked up at him.

"Hey, you and Dillon aren't the only people who are dating these days."

I shook my head. "Mackenzie and I are just friends."

"Whatever you say. Still, she's hot, nice, not a bitch, and anything you can do to make Sanders feel like shit makes me happy." He gave me a two-fingered salute and headed off to his bedroom.

"It seems I'm not the only one who thought you and Mackenzie were dating."

I shrugged at Nessa's words. "People can believe what they want. Doesn't make it correct."

"Maybe. Well, I need to get back."

"Are you sure? Are you okay driving home?"

"It's not snowing. It's just super cold. I'll be fine. Thank you for worrying about me."

"I always worry, Nessa. You're my best friend."

She smiled and shook her head.

"Goodbye, Pacey. Let me know when the party is."

"Of course. I'll need my best girls there." Nessa gave me an odd smile and shook her head. I froze, absorbing my words, and cursed myself. One of my best girls was gone. Forever. Damn it. Nessa held up her hand when I reached for her.

"No. The best girls are the ones that live in the house

now. And will always be Corinne, though she's going to be there rolling her eyes at us. Okay?" she said quickly. I nodded.

I walked her to her car, made sure she drove off safely and swallowed hard.

None of us were doing very well at this whole healing thing.

But we'd find a way. I wasn't sure what else we could do.

My phone buzzed as I walked inside. I saw it was a call, not a text.

I answered. "Well, hello, Mackenzie."

"Thank you for the flowers," she whispered into the phone.

I jogged up the stairs and tried to hold in a cough, annoyed with myself for being so short of breath.

"Are you okay, Pacey?"

"Yeah, just a little sinus infection. It's going away, but I have to finish out my antibiotics."

"It's been a week since we last saw each other on the date. You didn't look sick."

"You don't have to look sick to have a runny nose. I'm fine. It's why I kept my distance in class," I added.

Mackenzie went silent for a moment, and I wanted to reach through the phone and hold her, tell her that I was an idiot.

"I probably should have told you that so I didn't sound like an asshole. I blame the fever."

"Pacey, if you were sick, you should have told me. I thought you hated me or something."

"No, I could never hate you, Mackenzie. I got you flowers, didn't I?"

"I thought it was because you were saying, 'Thank you for crying on me, now I never want to see you again.'"

"Love..." I whispered.

"I'm fine. But you need to tell me exactly what happened this week, or I'm going to get angry."

I pinched the bridge of my nose then cursed because it hurt. "I started feeling sick the day after our date. I figured it was just a sinus infection. Or a cold. It wasn't too much. I've been on antibiotics because my doctor wants me to be careful. I'm fine, not contagious, and I didn't get anyone else sick. But I still wanted to be careful, so I sat away from you and everybody else. I kept coming in late because I felt like shit, and I didn't get a chance to tell you. And then, classes were difficult, and I forgot to text because of the aforementioned illness. I'm sorry I'm an idiot. Please forgive me."

She paused. "Are the flowers to say forgive you or thank you?"

"Thank you for the date, and please forgive me for not sending them sooner and for being a fool. Whatever you need them to be. Please don't hate me."

She sighed again, and I leaned into the couch in my room. "I'm not going to hate you. I don't. I only hate one person, and even then, I don't think I care enough to truly hate him anymore. But thank you for the flowers. And I hope you're feeling better. You really should have told me. I could have made you soup."

"Both Dillon and Tanner did. It helps that they both cook."

"I'm kind of jealous," she teased.

"Next time I'm sick, you can come over and eat their soup."

"I would say that sounds like a plan, but I don't want you to be sick."

"That would be a blessing."

"Thank you again for the flowers," she whispered.

"You already said that. A few times."

"I know. I'm just not good at this whole thing."

"And what is this whole thing?" I asked, wondering why I kept teasing...pushing.

"That's just it. I have no idea. But I had fun. I don't know what I'm doing, but I had fun. So, thank you for taking me out to dinner. It was nice going out with somebody I didn't know everything about. Or...you know what I mean. Since I didn't technically know much about Sanders either."

I let out a small growl. "Let's stop saying his name. It gets me all growly. Tanner's worse, but I can growl."

"You know what? Deal."

"I would ask you what you're wearing, but I don't want to come off too cliché."

She laughed, exactly how I wanted her to.

"I'm sorry for crying in front of you and on you."

"I didn't mind. You needed to get it out."

"And I did. And I feel oddly better. I know I'm not a hundred percent, but who knows if I ever will be. But I do feel so much better."

"Good." My head hurt, and I knew I'd probably have to go to sleep soon. "Now, for the next part of your rebound..."

She sputtered into the phone, and I laughed. "I can be your rebound guy. We can study together, be friends. I'll be anything you need. And we don't have to have sex, Mackenzie Thomas."

She was so silent that I was afraid the call had dropped, but I could still hear her breathing.

"You just laid it all out there, didn't you?"

"I think the whole point of my statement is that I'm not going to lay it all out there," I joked.

"Oh good, a penis joke. At least I'm back into the world of norm. What are you going to get out of this? Seriously. Can you have a rebound without sex?"

"I guess we could have sex if that's what you want," I said and ignored the way my dick hardened against my zipper.

"Oh, well, uh...."

"Thank you for that. I feel so invigorated."

"Pacey," she warned.

"Seriously. You and me. We'll be friends, study partners, and our version of a rebound."

"And no sex? No romantic feelings or craziness that will hurt both of us in the end?"

I swallowed hard and wished I could see her face when I answered.

"Of course, Mackenzie. Maybe it's time for both of us to settle down in our ways and make our version of what we need."

"It sounds crazy, but it also sounds perfect."

"And it sounds like a deal," I whispered.

I hoped to hell I wasn't making a mistake that would end up hurting us both in the end.

SEVEN

Mackenzie

MY HANDS CRAMPED, BUT THE NOTES WOULD BE worth it. I loved this class. I might be a nerd, a geek, a dork. All of the labels others needed to put on me, but I didn't care. This class was perfect for me and I was happy.

This was one of the math classes I was taking without Pacey, but I wouldn't allow myself to miss the fact that he wasn't there. He had another class to work on, and I planned to focus on this and enjoy myself. Which was an odd thing to say, considering I was writing down complicated equations for a math class, but my parents had always thought I was weird. And, honestly, they weren't wrong.

The guy behind me kicked my seat again, though he would likely tell me it was just an accident. I held back a small growl—we were in class, after all—and ignored him. I could hear him whisper to his friends behind me, and I disregarded that, too. I was having fun. This was my favorite class. I would be working with this professor for the summer, and it would hopefully propel me into my future.

I wouldn't allow Hunter Williams, III in all his asshole glory to annoy me.

He did not rule my life.

The fact that he was friends with Sanders notwithstanding.

I wouldn't allow my ex to take up space in my mind, either. Today was all about math, happiness, and then a meeting with Dr. Michaels. Everything would be wonderful.

"Now you have your homework from your syllabus. Make sure that's done appropriately. It's due on Monday. Good luck." Dr. Michaels finished his speech, and everybody went to put away their materials.

I carefully stuffed my notebook into my bag with my laptop. He preferred for us to take notes manually, but sometimes he wanted us to take them electronically. We needed to get into the new age, which was funny coming from that man. He lived in the ripe old age of misogynistic evilness. I planned to ignore that, though. Because I needed to work with him, and I was stronger than his petty sexist bullshit.

"Have fun at your meeting, Mac," Hunter said as he strode away, his friends beside him.

In most television shows and worlds, the math nerd wouldn't also be the bully, but they would be wrong. Because Hunter was the worst kind of bully. I had known him since we were kids. He had always been Sanders' friend, and when he chose the same college track as I did, I assumed it was because fate hated me.

I wasn't always so focused and centered on my universe. Hunter was a jerk, thought the world revolved around him, and was the reason I hadn't been valedictorian. He had gone to the principal, and they had unearthed an arcane rule that said Advanced Placement Spanish couldn't count towards AP credits. Oh, I could take the AP test and hopefully test out to get credits for college, and it would look great on my transcripts, but I couldn't add extra decimal points to my GPA. I hadn't known that. No one had. My advisor had even pushed me towards taking AP Spanish because I wanted to. And because it would help me in my career and in my life. It was the one AP class that I'd really wanted to take, and I had been lucky it had fit into my schedule.

They were going to look into it in the years to come, but because I had lost out on that 0.1, Hunter had ended up beating me for valedictorian. I had been the salutatorian instead. The girl who didn't give the speech, the second-best, and the one that everybody looked at with pity. Because everyone thought I must have cheated to get my way before they took everything from me. It couldn't have been Hunter who cheated. No, to them, I had been the one to break the rules. And Hunter had been cast in the light of the savior. He had almost been maligned and kicked out of his rightful place as heir to the throne.

I wasn't bitter or anything.

Much.

But that was just who Hunter was.

He constantly did things to make sure that he got the

best of everything, even if he had to step on people along the way.

Maybe that rule was right. Perhaps no one had seen it, and my advisor had pushed me in the wrong direction. It hadn't been malicious on her part—at least I hoped it hadn't. But I had been screwed, nonetheless.

And Hunter made sure that everybody knew he had beaten me. Said he always did.

But not today. Today, I would take my step in the right direction. Finally.

So, I ignored Hunter Williams, III.

The asshole.

"Ms. Thomas, if you'll meet with me in my office?" Dr. Michaels said, and I nodded.

"Of course," I replied aloud.

Hunter smirked, but I ignored him. I wasn't being sent to the principal's office. This was a planned meeting. I sat in front of Dr. Michaels and tried to rein in my excitement. Today was the day.

I would sign the papers and work towards my program. My senior year would be all about my thesis, and I needed my advisor to make that work. But my junior year was when I could choose which advisor to work with. I had already decided, and Dr. Michaels and I had an understanding. Today, that would be cemented. I would also work on the dates for my internship. I had been planning this since freshman year, and Dr. Michaels knew it. I was setting my sights high and knew that things would work out. They might not do so in my personal life, but I was moving past that and finding my future.

And this was only part of that.

"Ms. Thomas," Dr. Michaels began, and I smiled, but not too brightly.

"Hello, Dr. Michaels. I really enjoyed your lecture today."

"Of course," he muttered, looking down at his notes.

"And thank you for meeting with me," I began again, trying to think of what else to say. This would be a difficult semester if it turned out like this, but I would figure it out.

"Anyway, I suppose we should just get started."

Excitement bubbled up within me, and I did my best not to bounce in my seat.

"Of course. I cannot wait to get started. I have so many ideas for where I want to go, but I know that my senior thesis will be fantastic, what with working with you. We'll be able to work together, and I'll learn so much. Thank you."

He gave me a kind smile, but it didn't reach his eyes. A slight edge of worry slid through me.

"Well, Ms. Thomas, that's what I need to talk to you about."

I froze, unnerved at his tone. "Oh?" I asked, trying not to sound as if I were shaking inside.

"As you know, we hadn't made any final decisions yet. And with the way the budget is, I'm only allowed to have one student this year."

"I see." I didn't, but it seemed like the best thing to say.

"And though you are a strong candidate, I decided to go in another direction."

"Excuse me?" This couldn't be right. This slot was mine.

"I know you seem to think we had an understanding, even as early as last semester, and I'm sorry to have led you astray. But this is business. You'll need to learn to toughen up. Be a man about it."

"Be a *man* about it?" I whispered.

He rolled his eyes and floated his fingers in the air. "Or a woman. Whatever you need me to say that's more politically correct. As I said, I've gone in another direction. You're a strong candidate, but you're not what I'm looking for," he repeated. "You're going to land on your feet. You always do. You'll be able to find your program and internship pretty easily, most likely. There are other classes out there that you can focus on. Maybe something not so difficult as mine. I'm a taskmaster, and I need someone who will be up for it."

I sat there, my hand shaking, everything breaking inside.

This couldn't be happening. That *understanding* we'd had, had been Dr. Michaels saying outright that I was getting the program and internship and that I didn't need to look elsewhere. And I hadn't wanted to. This was the path I wanted to take. I had done the research. I had taken a year to go through everything that I could to pick this one. I wasn't headstrong and blind to my faults or his, but I knew this was what I wanted. And he had promised it to me. Now, he was tossing it all away.

Another sick wave slammed into my stomach and twisted my insides.

"This can't be true. We already talked about this. We were going to work together."

"You need to get things in writing."

"But...I had..."

He shook his head. "That's something you'll learn as an adult. And that's fine, you'll learn. Maybe pursue something a little softer. A little less strict and complicated for you."

That put my back up, and I raised my chin. "Excuse me? I'm your best student. I have been all year and in the class last year. You know that."

"You're not my best student. You try hard, and you work hard, but with others, it comes naturally. It's understandable, though. Not everybody's cut out for this. Please don't make a scene. I hate when people make scenes."

"Oh," I whispered, trying not to scream. He didn't mean just people. He clearly hated women. He resented that they *made scenes*, at least in his opinion. Disliked that I wasn't conforming to his ideals.

"Who took my place?"

"It was never your place, Ms. Thomas. I don't understand why you keep thinking that way. But if you must know, it was a bright student that I have high hopes for. Mr. Williams."

I swallowed hard, tears pricking the backs of my eyes. Not because I was sad or truly upset but because I was so fucking angry. And when I got angry, I cried.

That would likely make me a weepy woman in his eyes, so I refused to let myself break down. I blinked back the tears, hoping he didn't see them, and fisted my hands in my lap.

"I wasn't aware he was looking towards this area of expertise."

"It seems you were unaware of many things. Now, I don't need you to make that scene of yours. Just know that this is not personal. I need you to focus on finding an advisor. It will not be me. Please close the door on your way out and remember that you have homework."

"I...there's nothing I can do?" I asked, sputtering now.

"No. I've made my decision. You would do well to remember that college isn't like high school. You don't get everything you want just by smiling and pretending that you're going to get it. You need to work hard, and you need to be prepared for disappointments. Now, again, close the door on your way out."

I stood on shaky legs and raised my chin, just like Pacey had told me to do that one night, and I walked away from my dreams. Yet again.

Hunter stood in the hallway, smirking.

"Oh, look at you, disappointed again."

"I hate you," I whispered. And I hated myself for even saying those words. Because I shouldn't hate him. I shouldn't even think about him. Why was he here? Why was he always doing this?

"Aw, poor little buttercup. Now I'm going to talk with my advisor. Good luck finding yours this late in the game. You know, for someone who likes to plan so much, you sure do seem to have nothing in the end. I kind of like it. And since you're not with Sanders anymore, if you're ever looking for a little retreat, a way to get that stick out of your ass? Just call me. Bye, buttercup." He sauntered into the room, closing the door behind him. All I could do was stand there, feeling like I was going to throw up.

"This can't be happening." My hands shook, but I ignored it. I needed to get out of there. I needed to go somewhere. I had class in an hour, and maybe if I just went about my usual routine, things would make sense again because nothing made sense now.

I had gone into college with a plan. It had adjusted as time went on, as I learned more, but I had checkboxes and lists. Sanders and I were in love. We were going to get married after college and start a family after grad school. We would be together. Lean on each other during hard times. We would always have one another. And yet, he had thrown it all away. For a blowjob. Because I hadn't been enough.

I had plans with school, my future, the path I wanted, and the advisors I needed to get into the grad schools I desired.

And I had worked hard to make all that happen. It hadn't been all in my head. It hadn't been a dream. Dr. Michaels had promised me that internship and the advisor position. And then he had taken it away—to give to Hunter.

My apparent archnemesis. I wasn't supposed to have a fucking archnemesis. Those kinds of things weren't supposed to exist in the real world.

Bile filled my throat, and I swallowed hard and tried to go about my routine. My day-to-day would save me. It was the only thing that I had left. And what a sorry state that was.

I went to the coffee shop, the one with the three stories that all of my friends loved, and ordered a chai latte, figuring maybe it would settle my stomach. Something had to.

They called my name, and I smiled at the barista, wondering if the tears were actually falling from my eyes or if I just feared they were. She gave me a sad look, and I figured that yes, I probably looked as if I were losing my mind.

Maybe because I was.

I turned around and nearly tripped over my feet. Sanders sat on the corner couch, coffee in hand, his arm wrapped around a girl. Not the one who had been on her knees with her mouth wrapped around his cock that night. This girl had blue, blond, and black hair. She was gorgeous. And she seemed happy.

And so did Sanders. He looked carefree. Like he was comfortable.

And I wanted to cry harder. I wanted to scream. I wanted to do something. Anything.

But he looked *happy*.

He hadn't looked happy in our last months together. He'd looked stressed. I'd thought maybe it was school, but perhaps it'd been me. He had cheated on me, after all. Maybe it was all my fault. Perhaps I had been the one to do all of this. Had pushed him to his decisions.

Maybe he hadn't wanted this path, and that was my fault, too.

He didn't see me, and I didn't want him to. I turned and walked out of the building, knowing that I needed to change something about my present situation. But everything had fallen from me, and I didn't know where to go.

Everything crashing around me wasn't the track I had set myself on, and it wasn't what I thought my future would be.

I sipped my latte and burned my tongue, letting out a hollow laugh.

Nothing was working.

Lost didn't even begin to cover how I felt.

And yet, what was I supposed to do now?

"Mackenzie?" I looked over at the sound of Pacey's voice and quickly wiped the tears from my face.

"Oh, hi," I said. "Hi, Nessa. Pacey." The two came over, and I smiled up at them both. "It's good to see you."

"Why are you crying?" Pacey asked as he wiped some tears from my face.

I looked down at the wetness on this thumb and shook my head. "Long day. I don't want to make a scene."

"Mackenzie, what's wrong?" Nessa came up and squeezed my hand. I looked at them both, swallowed hard, and rolled my shoulders back. I was not going to cry in front of them. Not more than I already had. I wasn't going to cry in front of anyone. I would be fine.

"A shitty day. Guess I need to go do my homework or something. I need to focus."

Pacey tilted his head, studying my face. "Nessa and I were headed back to my place to study. Do you want to join us?"

I looked between them, saw Nessa's smile and Pacey's, and shrugged. "I have class, but maybe after?"

"Of course," Pacey said. "Join us. We can talk. Okay?" He cupped my face again, wiped my tears once more, and I nearly leaned in to him. But I shouldn't because he wasn't mine. We might joke that we were rebounds, but that wasn't our plan. I didn't have one. And that was the problem.

I nodded, and they walked away. Once I lost sight of them, I wondered what I was supposed to do.

Maybe not having a plan would be my new plan. I could fall into existentialism and wonder what I was supposed to be.

Who I was supposed to be.

Or maybe I could just pretend.

I had gotten good at pretending, after all. Now, I would excel at it.

EIGHT

Mackenzie

I PUSHED MY HAIR FROM MY FACE AND KNOCKED ON the door to the boys' home. I had been here once since breaking up with Sanders, but it hadn't occurred to me that when I agreed to come over and study with Pacey and Nessa, that I would be coming back to *this* place. For some reason, it didn't connect in my head that it was also Sanders' old place.

But I wouldn't let it bother me. It would be great. Nothing was going to rattle me today. Nothing more than it already had, anyway.

The door opened, and Pacey stood there, a raised brow on his face.

"Mackenzie, love. Why do you look like you're ready to bolt again?"

"Oh. What?" I said and cleared my throat. "Nothing," I added quickly. He shook his head.

"It's not nothing. It's you looking ready to heave the contents of your stomach all over my doorstep. Not quite the sight I wanted to see upon coming into your presence."

I sighed and shook my head. "Thank you for telling me I look horrid. I'm not ready to throw up. At least, I don't believe I am. I just realized that I haven't been inside the house, other than that one time to drop something off, since...you know, the *incident*."

Pacey cursed under his breath. "Damn it. I hadn't thought about that. Shit. Should we go to your house to study? Or somewhere else?"

I shook my head and tried to smile. "No, this is fine. I'm going to get over this. Today will not break me."

More than it already had.

He gave me a sad look. "Mackenzie."

Tears pricked again, and I cursed myself. "Stop. I'm fine. Let's study and pretend that everything's okay."

"If you have to pretend, then it's not okay. Are you going to talk to me? Tell me what happened today?"

"I guess I'll have to because I need someone to help me, and I think you're the best person for the job. A friend."

"Okay, I can do that."

"Why are you guys standing out on the porch?" Nessa asked as she came forward. "Is everything okay?"

"Everything's going to be great. I just need to make a plan."

"A plan sounds good. Sounds like something you would say."

I smiled at Pacey and rolled my shoulders back. "And

after studying, I could probably use a drink. But not before. Because I can't study while drunk."

"A single drink would get you sloshed?" he asked, and I winced.

"Oh, when I start drinking today, it's going to be more than a single drink," I said sagely.

His brows winged up. "Good to know. Well, we're stocked. Just let us know when you're ready," he said softly.

"Sounds like a plan. So, we're studying in your living room?" I asked as I walked in, my chin held high but my lip a little wobbly.

I noticed Pacey and Nessa give each other looks, but I ignored them. I was fine. I wasn't going to have another panic attack or stress out beyond all recognition. They didn't need to worry about me.

Much.

I sat down on the couch and put my backpack on the table.

"So, what are we studying today?"

"Before you open a textbook, you're going to tell me what the hell is wrong," Pacey ordered as he sat down next to me. Nessa looked like she wanted to sit down with us on the couch but shook her head and went to sit on the chair next to me instead.

I figured I had taken her seat, and I moved to get up.

"No, sit down, talk to us," Nessa said softly.

I quickly wiped the tears from my face, annoyed that I was crying again.

"Things are fucked up," I said.

Pacey studied me. "I would assume so. Please expand on that notion."

"Well, it all started after class today," I said and explained about my professor, and about the internship, and even Hunter and the whole valedictorian mess so they understood.

Nessa's eyes widened even more as I continued.

Pacey, however, glowered, his hands fisting on his lap as he took a deep breath.

"That asshole did what?" he asked, and I sighed.

"Which asshole are you talking about? Hunter or Dr. Michaels?"

"Either one at this point," he growled. "I was talking about Dr. Michaels, but yes, let's also discuss the asshole that is Hunter."

"Hunter doesn't matter. He never has. He inserts himself into my life and was always there because of Sanders." I paused. "I should have known that Sanders was a piece of shit because he continued to be friends with Hunter, even after the whole valedictorian thing happened. He said he couldn't just leave his friend because the guy got valedictorian. He didn't even really care about the fact that it had been stolen from me, even if it was because of a rule nobody had known about. He didn't have my back there, and I should've known."

"Mackenzie," Pacey said softly and held my hand. "Stop. It's not your fault. You followed your advisor. You thought you were doing everything right, and you still made it into university with a full-ride."

"I did," I whispered. "But it's the point of the thing."

"Oh, I believe you. I understand. But you're fine. You don't need to worry about what Hunter did. Though

Hunter should worry about what he's doing because I want to kick his ass."

"I'll hold your coat for you," Nessa said, nodding. "He doesn't get to just change his mind like that, right? I mean, the professor. What did Hunter do to make him pick him?"

"Well, first off, Hunter has a penis," I said, and Nessa rolled her eyes.

"Excuse me?" Pacey said.

I narrowed my eyes at him. "Like you haven't noticed."

"That Hunter Williams, III has a penis? I haven't seen it."

I blushed and shook my head. "That's not what I meant. I mean, you must have noticed how Dr. Michaels treats people. He likes guys better than girls. He doesn't believe women should be in the hard sciences. Thinks they should be in the squishy ones if in science at all."

"Hard and squishy?" Nessa asked.

Pacey groaned. "It's an archaic comparison in which only women are allowed to be in biology and the softer sciences that are warming and more like homemakers. And that men are supposed to be in the hard-thinking, analytical branches of science. That is if women are allowed in science at all."

"Exactly," I agreed. "It's ridiculous. But it's so ingrained in the industry that even I was starting to think along those lines when I first started college. I was wrong. The internal misogyny that comes with just being in STEM or any school of thought at this point is ridiculous. I'm sure you have to deal with it in your classes."

"Oh, yes, because men write hard literature, and women

write fanciful nonsense. I understand. And it's ridiculous. So, Dr. Michaels chose Hunter because he has a penis."

"That sounds about right. I mean, Hunter is brilliant, I'll give him that, but he's also a jerk. And always gets what he wants. And treats me like shit. And I hate it. And now, he's taking away everything and ruining my plans. Well, not everything. Sanders took part of my future plans away, but Hunter's taking away my choices, and my schedule, and everything that I worked for. I hate him. And I hate the fact that he's even taking up space in my mind. Because he shouldn't."

"No, he shouldn't," Pacey said, shaking his head. "And I'm sorry. Do you know what you're going to do?"

I pressed my lips together and shook my head. "No, and that's the problem. I don't know. I have lists of what the others are planning, but not everybody can have more than one student. And pickings are slim."

"It can't be that someone doesn't end up with an advisor, so they can't graduate," Nessa added. "Because that's ridiculous. How is that fair?"

"Everyone will get an advisor, but if I don't find the specialty I want, I'll end up in a field that I'm either not prepared for, or something that's not going to look good on my transcript if I want to focus in a certain area of study for grad school. This can really hinder everything, and I'm pissed off."

"You should be," Pacey said. "I wish there was something I could do, but even I need a minor thesis to get mine done, and I don't know if my professor's taking on anyone else."

I shook my head. "I have a meeting with Dr. Jackson later," I said.

Pacey's smile widened. "Good. Is she taking on more?"

"I don't know. But she's meeting with me, at least, and I have to count that as something. It's not exactly the four-year plan that I wanted," I said.

"No, it isn't, but it's somewhere close."

"Dr. Jackson's your professor?" Nessa asked, leaning forward.

Pacey nodded. "Yes, and she's wonderful. I know she already has two major students, and I'm her minor one. Maybe she'll take another."

"I hope so. There are a couple of others on my list, but everything's filling up so quickly. Because we've all been working towards this for how many years now? And now I feel like I'm starting over from scratch. This isn't where I want to be."

"I'm sorry," Pacey said again, softly.

"Me, too," I replied, staring at him. He just looked at me, and I felt like I could breathe again. Like everything would be okay, somehow. How could he do that? With only a look, one breath, I felt as if I could find my feet.

Nessa's phone buzzed, and I pulled myself away from Pacey's gaze and blushed, having forgotten that she was even there.

That wasn't a decent way to act like a friend.

"Crap. It's my project partner," she muttered. "I have to write a book this semester," she muttered.

My eyes widened. "A book?"

"Yes, but you have to write it with a partner. Where you're critiquing, and you guys turn in the same project. It's a ridiculous class, and I hate it. Plus, my person works full-time and is going to school full-time. I like them, they're brilliant, but they have like thirty minutes at a time where we can actually work together." She shook her head. "So, I need to go meet them. I'm sorry."

"Thank you for sitting and listening to me. I'm sorry I cut into your study time."

She looked between Pacey and me and shook her head. "No, this is exactly what we needed to do." She leaned down and kissed me on the top of the head and then did the same to Pacey. He rolled his eyes, even as she blushed.

"Well, on that awkward note, I'm heading out."

With Pacey walking her towards the door, she left, and I settled back into the couch and looked at my textbooks.

"I don't know if I'm ready to study."

"Come on up to my room," Pacey said, and my brows lifted.

"Excuse me?"

He smirked, but his eyes were kind. "Miles has his study group coming in about ten minutes, and they're going to be loud and obnoxious. Not because Miles is, but because of who he works with. We're going to make a proposal for you, and we're going to need quiet to do it. So, come on up to my room. I promise not to do anything nefarious. Unless you ask."

I swallowed hard and pressed my lips together. "Oh," I whispered.

"Well, that's nice to hear. Come on." He helped me pack up my books, did the same with his, and then led me up to his bedroom.

This was so odd, but it shouldn't be. I had been in this

hallway countless times before with Sanders. I had even followed Dillon into his bedroom with a box before as a surprise for Elise. But here I was, walking into Pacey's bedroom.

Pacey didn't have the largest room in the house, but he had the next biggest size. He had a large, king-sized bed, along with a small sitting area, and the bathroom looked gorgeous.

"You could fit three people in that tub." My face heated.

"I think Tanner may have tried in his tub, and it might not have worked out," Pacey said with a laugh.

"Did he ask to borrow your tub?"

"Yeah. Uh, no, and nobody's having sex in that tub but me."

And now I was thinking of Pacey naked in that tub, having sex with some random girl. I pushed that thought from my mind.

"Oh," I whispered.

"Yes, oh. I suppose we should stop talking about sex since that's not going to be part of our whole rebound."

I whirled on him, my eyes wide. "Really? You're just going to blurt that out like that?"

"I figured it's time that we try."

"Try what?"

"Saying what's on our minds. Let's get you through this plan, and then maybe work on some homework."

"Yes, that would probably be good."

He stepped forward and brushed my hair from my face. "What is on that mind of yours, Mackenzie?"

I swallowed hard, shivering at his touch and telling myself that this was silly. I was in a weird place, and me wanting Pacey like this was wrong. This wasn't in our plans, wasn't in the cards. And yet, since when had my plans actually worked?

"I was thinking about you naked in that tub," I said softly, and Pacey's eyes widened, his pupils going wide.

"Oh? Well, if I'm honest, I was thinking about you naked in that tub with me. Is that wrong?"

I swallowed hard, shaking my head.

"I don't think so. But I thought we weren't going to do the whole sex thing."

He cupped my cheek, his thumb running along my cheekbone. "We don't have to. Or we can be friends who lean on one another when we want. I want to be your friend, Mackenzie."

"You are, Pacey."

"Now, what do *you* want?" he whispered.

"I want to forget. Will you help me forget? Just for tonight?"

Pacey studied my face, and then he lowered his head and kissed me.

NINE

Pacey

I SHOULDN'T HAVE BEEN DOING THIS, BUT I couldn't stop. Mackenzie's lips parted beneath mine, and I groaned, tightening my hold on her as I deepened the kiss. She leaned in to me, her hands moving to my chest. But she didn't push me away. If she had, even barely, I'd have ended this mistake and tried to talk to her. Tried to do anything except learn her taste and find my salvation.

Her fingers dug into my chest, and I moved closer, needing her. This was wrong on so many levels. Mackenzie was my friend. *Only* my friend. And yet, I knew that to be a lie. I wouldn't be dreaming of her, aching for her if she were merely my friend. I kept telling myself that I only wanted to be in her life to be there for her, but that was also a lie. I just wanted to be there for her. I wanted to see her succeed because it brightened her smile and put an edge on everything she did.

But that wasn't what I was doing now.

Now, I was falling into my dream and pretending that this wouldn't irrevocably alter everything.

"Pacey..." she whispered against my lips.

I stiffened ever so slightly, catching my breath.

"Should we stop?" I breathed, looking into her eyes.

She licked her lips, then tilted her head back so she could see me better. "Maybe. But I don't want to."

Relief flooded me, even as a surge of adrenaline coursed through my system, making my hands practically shake with need.

"Are you sure?" I asked, and her eyes narrowed.

"I should be asking if *you're* sure."

"I don't want to hurt you, Mackenzie."

She smiled softly and leaned in to my hold. "You're not going to hurt me. This is what I want."

"Me? Or to just forget?"

She frowned, that little furrow between her brows adorable and oddly intoxicating. "You, first. Because you're my friend and because I want you. But maybe a little to forget."

I smiled. "I can work with that," and then I kissed her again.

She moaned, her hands raking down my chest. I pulled her closer and tugged her towards the couch. I sat down and dragged her onto my lap. She straddled me, the heat of her on top of my cock nearly sending me over the edge, even though we were both still clothed.

Her eyes widened, and then she smiled at me. I grinned right back.

"That's all for you," I said, nudging my erection up towards her.

She licked her lips and then rocked her hips before kissing me again. Her hair fell in a curtain around us, shielding us from the outside world as I kissed her, sliding my hands up and down her back. When they came to rest on her sides, and I squeezed her hips, she rocked again, and I moaned into her mouth, needing a moment to breathe.

"You're going to make me come right here just from your touch alone."

"Oh," she whispered. "I take it you're a fast starter?" she teased. I narrowed my eyes, tightening my hands on her hips.

"Not in the slightest. You do something to me. Now, I'm going to have to see how fast you go off the mark." I lifted my hips, pressing into her, against her heat. She shuddered and bit at my lip. I kissed her hard, my hands digging into her sides as I kept her in place, rocking into her. And then I let my hands roam up her body and under her shirt. She shuddered in my hold when I cupped her breasts, flicking her nipple over her bra. "Your breasts are the perfect size for my hands."

"Oh?" she asked, practically panting.

"They overfill my palms. I can't wait to taste them. Will you let me taste them?"

"I really need your mouth on my nipples right now."

I grinned, loving the way she looked down at me. "Any time you want to stop, you only need to tell me."

"I'm not telling you to stop. Please, keep going."

"I want this to be special for you. Good for you."

She frowned as she looked down at me. "This isn't my first time, Pacey."

"But it's your first time with me," I added. And it would be her first time with anyone but Sanders.

Understanding filled her gaze, and she nodded. "Just you and me here. I promise."

I didn't know if I quite believed that, but if that's what she needed to think, then I would go with it.

Because that's what I needed, as well.

I kissed her again and then tugged on the bottom of her shirt. She pulled back and raised her hands over her head. I tugged on her shirt and then pulled it off completely. She shuddered, and her skin pebbled.

"Cold?"

"I'm burning up," she said, and I smiled.

"And I'll take care of you." She was gorgeous, her pale skin nearly luminescent under the soft glow of my bedroom light.

She wore a pale, rose-colored bra that her breasts practically spilled out of. With each heaving breath, her nipples pressed into the lace, and so I leaned forward. I sucked one of her buds into my mouth. She let out a shocked gasp, and I flicked my tongue across it before I leaned back and gently pulled the lace away. Her nipple peaked, and I grinned before going back to lave at her skin.

"Pacey," she breathed.

I hummed against her, then sucked hard before I moved to her other breast, gently pulling the lace away again so I could lick and nibble at her skin. She tasted so sweet, was so soft, and I wanted more.

She rocked on me, grinding herself on my length, and I

moaned before I put my hands on her hips and made her freeze.

"I need a better angle," I said before pulling her down and kissing her hard again. And then I stood up, using my thighs to keep myself steady, and lifted her into my arms as I walked towards the bed. She let out a squeal and wrapped her legs around my waist, her arms banding tightly around my shoulders.

"You're going to drop me."

"I'll never drop you, Mackenzie. I promise." And then I dropped her on the bed. She let out a squeal, and I laughed before I hovered over her and kissed my way down her body. Her bra was a front clasp, and I undid the hook. Her eyes widened as the lace fell to either side of her. I leaned down, sucked one nipple into my mouth, and used my fingers on the other. She moaned, her whole body shaking. And when she began to writhe, I moved down her stomach, kissing along the edge of her pants. I tugged, and her eyes widened. I just grinned.

"We're only beginning," I whispered.

"Okay, sure," she said and then blushed.

I tilted my head and stared at her. "Are you okay with this? I'd love to taste you. You need to orgasm on my face."

"Well, I mean, I don't know if I like that. It wasn't, you know, something I did a lot."

I was going to kill him. Eviscerate the motherfucker.

"Are you telling me that Sanders didn't go down on you?" I asked, angry that I even had to bring up the guy's name.

She blushed again, slowly covering her breasts. And I hated Sanders for that, too.

"It just wasn't his thing."

"But I bet you that you went down on him often enough," I grumbled. I hadn't meant to say that out loud.

"Well, I like giving blowjobs," she said, ducking her head. "So, I didn't mind."

I clicked my tongue and shook my head. "I'm going to show you what you've been missing. And you are not going to be giving me a blowjob tonight."

Her eyes widened. "I just said I liked them."

"If I'm going to come, it's going to be in that sweet pussy of yours. After I make you come on my face. Next time, you can suck my dick."

Her eyes widened more. "You're saying there's going to be a next time?" she asked, licking her lips.

"I'm saying that next time can even be tonight if you want. I'm nowhere near done with you." Then I pulled at her leggings. They came off instantly, her ballet flats falling to the floor, her panties tucked into her leggings. She was naked before me, all sweet and soft, her pussy glistening.

"Perfect," I whispered. And then I knelt at the edge of the bed, positioned myself between her legs, and licked her clit. Her hips shot off the bed, her cunt coming closer to my face. I shoved her hips down and began to play. Her lower lips were swollen and ready for me, and I licked and sucked. I used two fingers to slowly play with her folds, just to tease. She moaned, writhing on my face. I looked up, and her hands were on her breasts, her eyes closed, her lips parted.

She looked like a goddess, and as God as my witness, I would make her come.

Because a man who didn't like going down on a woman

but wanted blowjobs? That was an asshole. And we all knew that Sanders was a fucking asshole.

I hummed again before I traced her core with my finger. Her eyes shot open as she looked down at me, her mouth forming an O. I met her gaze, latched my mouth to her clit, and speared her with two digits. She let out a shocked gasp, and I fucked her with my mouth and my fingers. And when her whole body tightened, she came, shouting my name.

It was bliss.

I used my free hand to squeeze my dick through my pants, willing myself not to come right there.

Because she was so beautiful when she came.

Her whole body turned pink, and her nipples hardened. I wanted to make her do it again.

So, I did.

I licked, sucked, and kept my mouth on her pussy, her folds wet and swollen.

And when she came again, I stood up and stripped off my shirt.

Her eyes widened, and she sat up, wavering slightly. I knew it was the haze of her orgasm. Her gaze raked my body, and then she reached out and tentatively put her hand on my abs.

"Whoa," she whispered.

"You say the sweetest things."

I lifted her chin with a pinch of my fingers and leaned down to kiss her.

I knew she could taste herself on me, so I kissed her harder, fucking her mouth with mine as her hands moved to my belt.

I pulled away and waved my finger in the air.

"No, no, no. My dick isn't going anywhere near your mouth this first time."

"You're no fun," she teased.

I grinned and pulled my pants down, taking my underwear with them. My dick slapped me on the stomach. I was so hard, I was surprised I didn't burst right there.

Her eyes widened even more, and she licked her lips.

"Should I say whoa again?"

"You really do say the sweetest things, Mackenzie mine."

She blinked at the usage of the phrase, but I ignored it. It'd surprised me, too. I went to my nightstand, got a row of condoms, and slowly slid one onto my dick.

"Get into the center of the bed, darling. I'm not done with you."

She scrambled to the middle of the mattress, and I moved beside her, kissing her softly and eagerly playing with her breasts.

"You're so beautiful," I whispered.

"You're not so bad yourself."

I rolled her onto her side, her back to me, and she let out a shocked gasp.

"Pacey."

"Let's try this first."

I lifted her leg, gently probed her entrance with the tip of my dick, and then slid home.

It seemed that Sanders liked it one way, and I planned to show her every other way I could. She was so tight in this position, her pussy squeezing my dick.

She let out a shocked gasp, and I began to move, slowly fucking her from behind. We stayed in that position for a bit, my hand on her side before I slid it up to her breasts and rotated us so she was on all fours in front of me.

"You're so fucking sweet, Mackenzie. If I'm not careful, I'm going to blow right here, and we've only just begun."

"Pacey," she breathed. I was on my knees behind her, and I spread her cheeks before I slid home again. My thumb brushed her back entrance, and she shivered. I grinned.

Maybe later, I told myself. Not tonight. Not when it felt like a first time for both of us.

I slid in and out of her, thrusting slowly, needing her touch, her moans, her taste.

And when I was there, I pulled out and twisted her to her back. She lay spread before me, her pussy wet, her breasts high and tight, and I slid into her again, this time bringing her knees up to her shoulders. She held on, and I fucked her hard, the bed shaking as both of us panted. I latched my mouth on to hers, needing her, and when she came again, squeezing my dick so tight I thought I might burst, I came, whispering her name, both of us shaking as we held each other.

And when it was over, our bliss finally receding, we lay there, my arms still around her, her body curled into mine. My dick was still hard, deep within her, and I knew that something had changed. And not just this. Something else.

She looked up at me, and I swore if she cried right then, I would break—for her, and myself.

But instead, she kissed my chest, nuzzled against me, and I held her.

And for once, I was at a loss for words.

TEN

Mackenzie

THE NEXT MORNING, I OPENED MY EYES AND TRIED
to remember exactly where I was. The room was unfamiliar,
and it took me a moment to realize that I was still in Pacey's
bed. With Pacey right behind me, his arm around my waist,
his naked body pressed against mine.

His very, *very* hard cock firm against my backside.

I stiffened, trying to calm my breathing so he wouldn't
know I was awake.

It was a lost cause.

"Good morning," he whispered, kissing my bare
shoulder.

I closed my eyes at the touch, squeezing my thighs
together at the sensation of his lips on my skin. I'd never felt

that before, and I didn't know what I was supposed to do about it.

Was it always like this?

What had I been missing out on all these years?

"You're probably freaking out a bit right now, so I'm going to speak, if that's okay."

I swallowed hard and nodded in his hold, hoping he could at least feel my answer since I couldn't talk.

"Elise and Dillon spent the night here as well, and therefore know you're here. They informed your roommates that you wouldn't be home. I spoke with them briefly to make sure everyone was aware that you were safe, but I didn't say anything else. For all they know, you slept on my couch after a long study session. However, they will probably guess the true nature of our evening. It is up to you what you tell them. I won't lie, but I will evade and allude to what is needed for your peace of mind. Tanner and Miles most likely know you are here as your car is still parked out front, but they won't bother you. What we did last night was perfectly normal, consensual. There's no need for discussion by anyone outside of this bed. And when you are ready to speak about it, I will be down in the kitchen making breakfast. First, however, I'm going to shower." He paused as my brain fought to catch up. "I had a wonderful time last night, Mackenzie. I know we need to talk, and we will before school. But I'm not sorry about what happened. I hope you know that."

Then he kissed my shoulder again, leaving me breathless as he strolled naked past the end of the bed and toward the bathroom. I watched his muscles flex as he walked, and I once again lost my breath at the sight of him. He was...beautiful. All lean lines and muscles. He had a few scars that looked surgical, but I couldn't tell what they were from at just a casual glance, nor could I learn their story from the feel of them under my fingertips. They weren't mine to know anyway.

This was just...casual, was it not?

It didn't need to be anything more than it was. I needed to keep reminding myself of that. I didn't need to stress and make a big deal of any of this.

Only I knew I *would* stress and make a big deal of it all.

The shower turned on, and I lay there covered by his sheets, wrapped in his scent and the memories of what had happened the night before. I honestly hadn't come here for this. I hadn't thought, even as my rebound as he jokingly called himself, that we'd ever do this.

And yet...

And yet, I couldn't stop thinking about it.

I didn't want regrets. I'd spent too much of my time living in regret already. I didn't want to continue down that path.

Only I wasn't sure what I was supposed to do. What should I say?

Things with Sanders had been so different. We had been each other's firsts. Young and inexperienced. And we had grown into one another and the sex we had together. It had been good, not great every time, but we'd had a rhythm.

Sex with Pacey was nothing like that.

The shower cut off, and Pacey walked out, a towel wrapped around his hips. He was still wet, and I swallowed hard, watching a droplet of water slowly pebble and run down his chest. He leaned over me, and I looked up at him, my eyes wide. He gave me a small smile and brushed my hair back from my face. "If you need to shower, I set out a towel for you. I'm afraid I don't have any clothes that will fit you, but I can ask Elise—though she might be in class right now. We don't have class 'til the afternoon, but they have morning ones."

I looked at the clock and blinked. "Oh," I whispered.

I was usually much more verbose and intelligent. But nothing else but that one word came to mind. He leaned down and pressed a kiss to my lips. "I'll see you downstairs."

"Oh," I said again.

"Yes, *oh*."

And then he grabbed his clothes, dropped his towel, and began to dress. I sat up, pulled the sheet over my breasts, and pushed my hair away from my face.

"You don't have a problem with nudity, do you?"

He grinned and looked down at his very hard cock. "You've already seen everything, love."

"I have. Um, we're going to talk over breakfast?"

"We probably should. Because we're friends, Mackenzie. And friends talk. Though I do make an excellent egg white scramble."

"I guess I could eat. I sort of skipped dinner," I said, lowering my head.

"Oh, we ate, just not what we needed to refuel." He winked as he said it, and I rolled my eyes. "Really? You're going to make a joke like that?"

"Anything to make you smile, Mackenzie." He tugged his shirt over his head, and I missed the sight of his muscles immediately. "I'll see you downstairs. Take your time. We've got this, Mackenzie. You don't need to stress out."

"That's easier said than done."

"I agree," he said with a hollow laugh. "I'll see you downstairs." And then he opened the door and left, leaving me sitting naked in his bed, the smell of sex all around me.

I'd had sex with Pacey Ziglar, and I'd loved it.

I had never orgasmed so many times in one night before. Even that time I'd bought a new vibrator and tried to see how long I could go.

Pacey was so talented with his hands, his mouth, with every inch of him.

And I swore that British accent nearly sent me over the edge all by itself.

He hadn't asked for anything in return. Sure, he had taken his share, came along with me, but he had given me so much more. I knew I didn't need to repay anything, that wasn't the type of person Pacey was, but I felt like I needed to do something. Feel something.

Only I wasn't sure what I was supposed to do.

I let out a breath and swallowed hard before I got out of bed. I brought the sheet with me, knowing it was silly since nobody else was in the house.

But, apparently, everybody now knew I had spent the night here. They knew that my rebound was now fulfilled, whatever that meant.

And I would have to face that, as well.

I grabbed my clothes and my book bag and made my way to his bathroom.

I looked at myself in the mirror and blinked. The mess on my head was the epitome of sex hair. It was naturally wavy, and I straightened it every time I blew it out, but I had a little more body at the roots now, and the curls were starting to come in at the ends. That meant I looked like a pinup girl with my hair falling around my face.

I wasn't sure if I liked it. I looked happy. Perhaps *sated* was a better word. I looked like maybe I was okay.

And I hadn't thought about Sanders at all, other than that first moment when I blushed and talked about oral sex.

For somebody having sex, I shouldn't be so embarrassed thinking or talking about it.

I would have to get better about that.

I was an adult, after all. I'd officially had more than one sexual partner.

I had been on birth control since I was sixteen, and we had used multiple condoms the night before. We had been safe. At least, I hoped we had.

Because we might've been safe physically, but I wasn't sure you could truly be safe emotionally when it came to sex. I didn't think I was a casual person. The one guy I'd been with before Pacey I'd had in my life forever. He was supposed to be my forever. At least that's what I had thought. And now he wasn't in my life, and he wouldn't ever be again. And I thought I was okay with that.

I wasn't the same person I had been before yesterday, nor was I the same woman I had been with Sanders.

Nearly two months had passed since I had broken up with Sanders, and I had completely changed in that time.

My life might be somewhat in shambles right now because I didn't know where I was going with things, but maybe, just maybe, I could be a different person. I could figure out who I was. But I couldn't be casual about it.

There was nothing casual about who I was, and I hoped Pacey understood that.

I looked in the mirror again, noticed the bruised and swollen lips, and I let the sheet fall. My nipples were still hard, a little darker than before as if swollen from Pacey's mouth. I had slight bruises on my hips from where his fingers had dug in as he pounded into me from behind. I knew he likely had bruises on his back and his arms as well because I had held on for dear life as we rode each other into oblivion.

It was the sweetest, softest, and yet hardest sex I had ever had in my life—and all at once.

Pacey was a conundrum, and I had fallen right into it. And now, I wasn't sure I wanted to get back out again.

I let out a sigh. I needed to get through my day. And we at least needed to have this conversation so I could move on to wondering what I was going to do next about everything in my life. And not just Pacey.

I went about my business and used the spare toothbrush he had. I hoped that it wasn't one he had for random girls he had over, but that would be none of my business. Maybe he just had spares for when he needed to replace his. I would go with that. After all, I did the same thing. I pulled out a brush from my backpack and ran it through my hair, and then piled it on the top of my head. I jumped into the shower, looked around at the gorgeousness of the stall, and wondered how on earth the guys could afford this place. It was stunning. Everything looked intricate and nearly antique.

I was a little jealous.

I turned on the tap, and it immediately began to steam. I smiled, letting the hot water soothe my aching muscles. I poured some of Pacey's soap into my hands and ran it over my body. It smelled just like him, that scent of sandalwood and man, and I pressed my legs together.

Now, I would smell like him all day after washing off the scent of sex.

Maybe this had been a mistake.

Not last night, but this moment.

I rinsed off and used the plush towel he had set out, wrapping it around my body.

I had a spare travel kit in my backpack because I never knew when I might need it, and quickly put on some concealer, mascara, and a little lip gloss. I didn't need to look perfect for the day, but I needed to look as if I had gotten more than two hours of sleep. Pacey had kept me up most of the night.

I needed to go back to my house later anyway to pick up my books and notes for the classes that I had, ones I had with Pacey. So, while I would have to do a slight walk of shame to my house in the clothes I had worn the day before, I wouldn't have to run into the school.

I tucked my underwear into my backpack and slid on my leggings without them. I put on my bra and tank top, a shirt over it, and called it a day.

I looked... different. A little more relaxed, maybe? No, I was still as high-strung as ever.

I honestly wasn't sure what I felt.

Maybe talking to Pacey would help.

I packed my bag and went downstairs, steeling myself for the inevitable conversation that I knew needed to happen, though I wasn't sure what I would say.

I was also afraid of who would be around because I didn't know everybody's schedule. For all I knew, there could be a gigantic study group of fifteen people I didn't know, and one or more of Pacey's roommates, staring, judging. Waiting.

And yet, when I went down to the living room and looked around, there was no one else.

"Everyone's at school. It's just us," Pacey said from the kitchen. The smell of coffee and something on the stove that smelled savory filled my nose, and I made my way to the kitchen.

"Oh," I said and cursed under my breath. "I know other words other than *oh*. Good morning," I said.

I stood next to Pacey, my hands on the kitchen island. He just smiled at me and then leaned forward and brushed a kiss against my lips. My toes curled in my shoes, and I swallowed hard.

"Hi," I whispered.

"I'm glad you can say something other than 'oh.' And, yes, everyone's gone. It's just you and me. Breakfast is ready. You made good time." He looked down at me. "And you look beautiful."

I snorted. "I look a little wrinkled."

"And yet, you're bright and sunny. I know I would hate you if I didn't like the way that you looked."

I snorted at that and then sat down on a bar stool as he put a plate in front of me.

"I only know how you like your coffee at the coffee shop, not here."

My eyebrows rose. "You know that much?"

"I've been with you a few times when you ordered. I know what you like."

"Oh," I said again and laughed. "I like coffee with cream and lots of sugar. I know it's bad for me, but I need it."

"No problem. I made tea for myself, but I did start a pot of coffee for you."

"I could have had tea. I like it."

He smiled. "I'll teach you the correct way to drink it, then."

"Tea snob."

"Maybe. It's the two halves of myself warring."

"Perhaps," I said with a laugh.

This felt easy. Like we would be okay. As if we hadn't ruined everything by going with this whole rebound plan that we didn't really plan for at all.

"Here you go," he said and set the cup in front of me. I licked my lips, then blew over the surface. "Thank you." I took a sip. It was the ideal temperature, the flavoring just right. "This is perfect," I said.

"Good to know. Now, eat. I'll sit next to you. We don't have to talk right now."

"Maybe we should," I said but took a bite. Flavor exploded on my tongue, and I groaned. "This is fantastic."

"Just a few things from the fridge mixed in with some egg whites. I'm not a fan of yolks unless I'm dipping toast in it—or it's deviled."

I laughed. "Same. Dippy eggs are the best."

"See, I knew we were right for each other." He winked, and I froze.

He let out a sigh and shook his head. "Well, that was awkward. Let's begin again," he said and took a bite.

"Begin speaking, or begin eating?"

"Both, but not at the same time. We do have manners, after all."

That made me snort, and I shook my head before I started eating again.

"Are you okay this morning?" he asked after a few moments of silence.

I nodded. "Last night was amazing, Pacey. I don't know how else to say it. I also don't want to stroke your ego."

"You stroked a lot more last night," he teased.

I rolled my eyes. "I walked right into that one."

"You did. I had a wonderful time last night, too. I'm glad it happened. I'm not going to regret it."

I shook my head. "I can't regret it either. I don't want to live my life full of regrets anymore."

"That's good," he said and leaned forward. "That's good to know."

"I just...what is this, Pacey?" I blurted and then stuffed my mouth full of breakfast.

He nodded, took a bite, and slowly chewed while I swallowed, trying to let my mind catch up with everything.

"You need labels, don't you?" he asked. But it didn't sound like he was judging, more as if he was clarifying.

I nodded. "Yes. I'm sorry. I know that it's cool to go without labels and find your way and just muddle through, but that's not me. I can't be *me* without labels. And if that means ours is just friends who had sex once and never talk about it again? That'll be what it is. Because I need those labels. Preferably color-coded," I added with a soft laugh at the end.

Pacey's eyes brightened. "I'm good with anything. But, yes, I can see that you need labels. And, honestly, so do I. I may not seem the type, but I'm not as cavalier with relation-ships as others might think. I wouldn't mind a label for us. And if I say...how about we just enjoy each other? That doesn't seem like enough."

"It is. But no cheating," I added. "No cheating at all. Oh, and a blowjob counts as cheating." I blushed and sipped more of my coffee.

"Of course. And I would never. And you and me, we can be our rebounds together. And date. Enjoy one another and see where it leads. Exclusively."

My eyes widened. "Because we need companionship."

"That's what you like," he whispered. And then he leaned forward and brushed a kiss over my lips. "We'll study, we'll kick ass with your new plan as you figure it out—and with my help if you need. And we'll be friends. Who occa-sionally have mind-blowing sex. But just with each other. That much I can promise you."

I smiled. "A friend. I could use that. A friend."

He kissed me again and then smiled. "A friend will help me do the dishes. And then you can head home if you need to pick up your books and things. I will see you in class. Because we have an exam coming up, and I need to kick ass on it."

I rolled my eyes, feeling more at ease than ever before. "Oh, no, I'm going to kick your ass on it. We're going to break the curve together."

"As long as you break it for that Hunter asshole."

I scowled. "Hunter Williams, III is a jerk. I hope he fails." My eyes widened. "That's not a nice thing for me to say but fuck it."

"We don't have to be nice all the time, Mackenzie. We're

allowed to have an archnemesis."

That made me snort. "You make me sound like I'm in a movie."

He shook his head. "Sometimes, people want to create a reality where there's a chance to change. But in the past two and a half years I have seen that kid, there is no changing for him."

"I've known him much longer," I said drolly.

"So, he can go fuck himself. Let's prove to your professor—and to Hunter—that you're amazing. Something I already know."

I warmed and smiled. I wondered what the hell I was doing.

Because we could assign the labels, say we were exclusive, but we still hadn't talked about what we really were. Friends with benefits? People sort of dating and finding out who they were?

Exclusivity was the label that I needed, though. So, it would have to be enough for now.

I just didn't know exactly what would happen from here.

But I couldn't focus only on Pacey. I needed to put that to the side and lean in to the exclusivity part that we spoke of. Because nothing else in my life made sense.

Not school, not the way that I felt with my roommates...nothing.

And the fact that it seemed that something else changed every time I turned around wasn't lost on me.

I needed to figure out what all of that meant.

And where I went next.

I only hoped I didn't hurt myself irrevocably in the end.

ELEVEN

Pacey

"Now, REMEMBER, WE JOKE THAT WE WANT TO solve for X, but that's only the beginning. We don't care about X. We care about all the other letters in the alphabet." The professor looked down at his watch and nodded. "And on that note, we'll call it a day. Your next assignment is already listed, and the supplemental paperwork is on the website. You know what to do. See you next week."

People started stuffing their backpacks and heading out of the classroom. I looked over at Mackenzie and raised a brow. "Well, that was enlightening," I deadpanned.

She rolled her eyes and took some final notes before packing everything up.

"By enlightening, you mean exhausting?" she whispered and then looked around to make sure nobody was listening.

The people behind us had already left, and the professor had gone with them, leaving his work on the board as if he didn't care. If I remembered right, he had another class on the other end of campus in less than thirty minutes. I didn't blame him for running out.

"We have a lot of homework this weekend, and I feel like we're not done yet," Mackenzie said, looking down at her planner.

"We never will be, but it's preparing us for our futures," I said, laughing.

"Whatever you say."

It had been three days since Mackenzie and I had slept together. We had done nothing more than kiss a few times on our way from class, the coffee shop, or home. The semester was gearing up, which meant there was little time for anything but getting to class. Each of us took a larger than average course load, and I had meetings with my advisor besides. I knew Mackenzie was working on figuring out her next steps.

I didn't know what we were doing, other than pretending that we knew what we were doing. However, I assumed that was how most college students lived these days. So, I counted it as something.

"Are you coming over this weekend to study?" I asked, helping Mackenzie with her coat. She gave me a small smile, and I grinned. We were figuring out who we were to each other, and I liked having her in my life. Even if we only ended up as friends, I was better for it. And that was an odd thing to think, wasn't it?

"I need to study. I'll probably be over, or you can come over to our house. But yours is much nicer."

I nodded, picking up my messenger bag and slinging it over my shoulder.

"Our house is pretty nice."

"I'm a little jealous, but that's fine," she said with a laugh. "I also need to work out my game plan with my advisors. I've done everything I can in the moments I've had to think about what I need to do. Now, I need to do it. I've emailed a few professors, but I need to email the rest and then just hope for the best."

"I hope Professor Jackson can help," I said.

"You wouldn't mind if I worked with your professor?" she asked.

"No, we work well together, Mackenzie."

"But we're already spending a lot of time together. I don't want it to be too much."

I scowled.

"It's not like with Sanders," I whispered, and her eyes widened.

"I wasn't even thinking that. Sanders and I didn't have a lot of classes together. Yes, we spent a lot of time together and did most things together because, hello, we were together, but we didn't even really study together. Not unless I needed him to study." She rolled her eyes. "I don't want to talk about him anymore."

"I shouldn't have even brought him up. I'm sorry." I leaned down and kissed her softly. Her eyes widened for a moment before she leaned in to me.

"You move fast, Mac," Hunter said as he walked past us.

"Ignore him," Mackenzie whispered, tugging on my jacket. "He's not worth it."

"Not even in the slightest. But I still hate that wanker."

"Oh, I hate him more. Don't you worry, he will always be on my I-hate list."

"Why am I not surprised that you probably have a list that's exactly like that."

"With washi tape and stickers and everything," she said, laughing.

We made our way out of the building, and I looked down at my watch.

"I have dinner with my dad tonight. Meet up tomorrow?"

"Of course. Are you going to be okay? It's just with him, right?"

"Yes, dear old Dad."

I had told her yesterday during our study break about my parents' upcoming divorce. It had slipped out, something I hadn't spoken about with anyone else yet. It surprised me that I had mentioned it, but it shouldn't have. Mackenzie was my friend. We might have slept together and could do it again, and I had just kissed her in public. I should be able to talk to her. Maybe not about everything because I wasn't sure about everything myself, but it was still something.

"Dinner tonight with Dad, dinner next week with Mom. Before they go back overseas to deal with the divorce. I think they're already learning how to alternate time with me. It's a little shocking how quickly that happened."

Mackenzie shook her head. "My parents are still together, though they fight a lot. I think it's because they like fighting," she grumbled. "I'm just sorry you're going through this. You shouldn't have to."

I shrugged, trying to pretend that the announcement of

my parents' divorce hadn't irrevocably altered my foundation. "They'll figure it out. I just hope to hell they don't pull me into the middle of it."

"Do you think your mom's going to stay in the country?"

"I don't know," I said, a little uneasy. "Mom's family's still here. My aunt lives in the area, and she's staying with her for now. I don't know what the plan is, and I don't think they feel free to talk to me about it."

"Is that going to alter your plans for after school?" she asked, though she wasn't looking at me as she said it. It was no secret that I still wasn't sure if I would stay here or go back to the UK for grad school. I had options. I hadn't had any true connections here before to make it worth staying, other than my extended family. But then moving in with the guys, making friends, meeting the girls, and now whatever this was with Mackenzie? That part might still be new, but everything else wasn't. I had more connections here than I thought possible.

"I don't know," I said after a moment. "If my mom ends up staying here, maybe I will, too. Or perhaps I will anyway, even if she goes back. I don't know yet. I will probably apply to many places, though. Because what if I get a full-ride to Oxford or Cambridge and not somewhere here. You never know what'll happen these days with funding the way it is."

"Don't remind me," she said and groaned. "If I don't get an advisor, they're going to place me with one who isn't even near my preferred field, and I'm not going to have any hope of getting into a decent grad school."

I brought her hand to my lips and kissed the back of it. "We'll figure it out. You're not alone in this. And not every undergrad is like ours, so it will be a different playing field for graduate school."

Her eyes warmed, and she smiled softly. "I guess you're right."

"Hey, you guys," Nessa said as she came up to us. Her gaze went to our clasped hands, and then her eyebrows shot up. "Oh. Well."

Mackenzie cleared her throat and pulled her hand away from mine. I let her, only because I didn't want things to be awkward. Nessa was my friend, and she and Mackenzie were roommates. This was the first time anybody had seen us out and about where they could put whatever label they wanted on us.

I wasn't sure how I should act either, which was different for me because usually I always knew.

"Hi, Nessa," Mackenzie said quickly. "How was your last class?" she asked, and Nessa just blinked between us.

"Good. The usual. So, this is a thing?" Nessa asked, looking between us. "Not that it's not awesome. I mean... yay. I just wasn't expecting it to be a thing, I guess. I'm sorry. Is that weird?"

She kept babbling, and I leaned forward and took her hands. Mackenzie smiled softly and looked between us. "We're taking it slow. We're figuring things out."

"Right," Mackenzie added. "I haven't seen you lately, so I'm sorry if this was a surprise, even though we're still just friends. All of us. Just friends," Mackenzie said, and Nessa smiled.

"You guys are cute. Stop freaking out. I mean, people are going to freak out because we like gossip, and it's going to go all over social media and group texts, but it's what we do.

Now, I need to eat because I skipped lunch thanks to cramming for an exam."

"You never cram for an exam."

"I do when the material's annoying as heck. Do you guys want to go get dinner?"

"I have dinner with my dad tonight, unfortunately."

"Oh, I'm sorry," Nessa said.

"I'm headed back to the house. I need to work on a few things. Did you drive? Do you need a ride?" Mackenzie asked.

"I rode in with Natalie, but sure, I'd love a ride home," Nessa said, smiling. "Have fun with your dad tonight," she added.

I smiled. "I'll try. Have fun. I will see you both tomorrow. There's a lot of studying in our future as exams are coming up."

"Don't remind me," Mackenzie said, and Nessa just shook her head. "Seriously, don't."

It would have felt awkward to lean in and kiss her goodbye, mostly because we didn't know what we were doing, even if we pretended to put labels on it, so I nodded my head at them and headed towards my car. Nessa and Mackenzie walked away, both of them talking rapidly about their days.

I was glad that Mackenzie had the ladies now. She had been living with some other girls who had all graduated.

I knew Mackenzie felt lost, as did a lot of us these days. I only hoped to hell she found her way soon. It was odd that I had joked about being her rebound. That way, she had someone to lean on. Yet, here I was, needing to lean on her—and wanting to. I wasn't going to think too hard on that. We had other things to focus on. But I could still want.

I reached my car and then drove towards the restaurant. Dad was staying at a hotel but had wanted to meet at a little bistro nearby. I liked the place. They served decent food, and it wasn't outrageously expensive. I was still on college money at this point. If I weren't taking so many courses to get the degrees I wanted, I would have a job—the same with so many of us. Dillon was my only roommate with a real job these days. I hoped it all worked out in the end.

I pulled into the parking lot. Since I didn't know what rental car my dad was using to know if he had arrived yet, I walked in. "Hello, I'm here for Ziglar, party of two."

The hostess smiled. "There's a Ziglar party of three. And the rest of your party's already here."

I blinked. "Oh, I guess my mum came with him. I wasn't expecting that. And you don't need to know that, sorry. Can you just point the way? I'll make my way over."

"No problem, honey," the older woman said. "They're right around the corner."

"Thank you," I said and walked towards the back.

I hadn't expected my mother to join us. I didn't think they would get back together because once my parents made decisions, they *made decisions*. It was still a good sign that she was here with him, though. Right?

I moved around the corner and blinked, wondering who the hell the brunette woman was sitting next to my dad. Her hair was in a complicated knot on the top of her head. She had a bright smile and wore glasses and a skintight dress.

She was also probably only about ten years older than me. If that.

Who the hell was this woman, and why was she draped over my father?

A ball of anxiety sank to my gut, and I swallowed hard.

Please, dear God, don't let this be what I think it is.

Please let this be a hooker for the night and not what it could be in truth.

My dad met my gaze and smiled. He patted the woman's hand, and she looked up at me and grinned.

"Pacey," my dad said. "I want you to meet Jessica."

"I didn't know we were meeting one of your coworkers today," I said, outright lying to myself.

My dad frowned. "Jessica, Pacey. Jessica already knows about you, but Pacey, my son, this is the woman I wanted to talk to you about." He squeezed her hand, and I stood there, not taking a seat.

"It's so good to meet you finally. Your dad's told me all about you."

"I, honest to God, have no idea who you are," I growled. There was no use trying to act civilly just then.

"Pacey," my dad snapped.

"No, I'm not going to do this. I have a lot of schoolwork to get to. I cannot deal with this right now."

"Pacey, sit down, don't make a scene."

"Who is Jessica, Dad?"

"Pacey," my dad breathed.

"No, tell me. Then I'll decide if I should sit or not."

My lungs hurt. I knew stress exacerbated my condition, so I wasn't going to let myself fall prey to it. But Jesus Christ, I couldn't breathe.

I tried to take a deep breath, but my lungs wouldn't work. My dad's eyes widened.

"Pacey, it's okay, you're fine. When's the last time you went to the doctor?"

"What's wrong?" Jessica asked, her eyes wide as she looked between us.

"I'm fine," I gritted out. "Dad, please don't tell me this is your girlfriend."

"I'm not going to lie to you."

"Seems you've been lying to me for a long time."

"Pacey, your mom and I drifted apart. We've been separated for a long while. Yes, this is my girlfriend, Jessica. I wanted you to meet her, and..." Dad cleared his throat. "We have news."

I blinked, black spots now dotting my vision before I could shake them away. I looked over at Jessica and saw that she only had water in front of her, not the wine my father had. I looked down at the slight bump showing in that skintight dress, then up at my dad.

"Nope, I'm not doing this. Not now." I turned on my heel and walked out.

I heard my dad shouting behind me, making the scene that he hadn't wanted. Still, I left.

Dear God. Not only were my parents getting a divorce—the two people that I thought could weather anything and had shown me that true love actually existed and all that other Hallmark and gross, gooey crap. They had been lying the whole time.

He had been lying the whole time.

And Jessica was pregnant.

I got into my car and pulled out of the parking lot before my dad could reach me.

I ignored the call from him, and as I hit end to block it, my phone app lit up on my car dash. I saw Mackenzie's name.

I could call her. I could lean on her. But not right now.

I needed to breathe. Had to think.

And I needed to figure out what in the hell I was going to do.

And wonder why Mackenzie, my friend, my rebound as we joked, was the one person I wanted to talk to just then.

Not my best friend, not my roommates, but Mackenzie.

TWELVE

Mackenzie

I scribbled as quickly as I could, trying to keep up, but I had a feeling that I wasn't the only one who felt lost. The first significant exam that would account for thirty percent of our grade was coming up at the end of next week, which meant everybody was scrambling. I had been keeping up with my homework and everything else I could with this class, even though it felt like the professor was racing to *teach*—in air-quotes—everything he knew would be on the test. I had a feeling we had spent so much time going over how he wanted us to learn that he'd forgotten how to teach us. But I wouldn't complain. Because I honestly didn't have time or energy to do it.

Pacey was at my side, writing as fast as he could, as well. This was honestly one of the only times in recent days that I could remember sitting next to him and not thinking about him in any way other than the guy I hoped took notes on anything I missed.

"Now, if you've done the reading, this should all make sense. If it's not making sense to you, that's not on me. That's you not wanting to use your book. I realize that many of you are used to taking the easy way out when it comes to homework, but you need to learn to study. You're adults. This is preparing you for the rest of your life. Now, I'll see you next time we have class. And I expect you to be better. Today was a disappointment." And with that, he turned and started erasing the board.

My eyes shot up. I risked a glance at Pacey, who blinked, and both of us went back to scribbling as many of the notes down as we could.

That this professor was erasing everything he had written and lectured on while his students were still trying to catch up was ridiculous. And if he caught us taking out a cell phone to take a photo of it, he'd fail us. It was right in the syllabus. I didn't know if that was legal, but I couldn't do anything about it.

I heard a snort from behind me, and I knew it was Hunter, but I ignored him.

I couldn't focus on him, not when I needed to flesh out the last equation. Thankfully, I recorded the final set of parentheses and shook out my hand as the professor nodded, then picked up his bag and walked out.

"Was that an X or a Y? Oh, God, or was it another Greek letter that I missed?" Pacey mumbled, and I smiled.

"It was a simple X. Thank the math gods."

"Compare notes when we get back to my place later?" he asked, a brow raised.

I let out a relieved sigh. "Yes. I'm so glad you're taking this class with me."

"Well, there are benefits to joining a class or two with you, although I can't use most of those benefits when we're in a classroom."

I blushed, cleared my throat, and quickly started putting everything away. People talked all around us, trying to share notes and figure out exactly what the last equation was.

I hated this class, and I was glad that it wasn't the focus for my future. Although if things didn't look up soon, I would end up with this guy as my advisor because I was running out of time and options for who could fit me in. He had a spot open. This would be my last resort.

Not something I wanted to worry about.

Yet.

I had a couple of meetings coming up in the next week to flesh out the rest of my plan. If those didn't work, I had a feeling I'd be studying and fleshing out my senior thesis with this guy.

I rubbed my temples and started out the door, Pacey right behind me.

"Coffee?" he asked.

I shook my head. "I'm meeting the girls for a late lunch at the house." I smiled softly, trying not to let my trepidation show. But Pacey could read my expression. It shouldn't surprise me that he was able to so quickly, and yet, it did.

"You'll be fine. You were friends with them before this. You don't need to be nervous."

"They were roommates for so much longer, though. It's

just an odd situation." Made odder by the fact that something was going on with Nessa, and I couldn't figure out what it was. She wasn't acting mean to me or ignoring me, but there was this...vibe I couldn't quite figure out. I knew there had to be a blatant reason, and figured I was missing the obvious.

I just needed to figure out what that was.

"I still can't believe you jumped in so quickly, Mac. Wasn't expecting it from you. Sure you weren't dating this guy before Sanders dumped your ass?" Hunter asked as he walked past.

I put my hand on Pacey's chest, not sure if he would do anything. He just raised a brow as he looked at me. "I'm much more civilized than that," he whispered, though his eyes were narrowed, and his jaw was tense.

"Let's just not get kicked off campus and out of school completely. You can kick his ass later."

Pacey smiled and took my hand off his chest, bringing my palm to his lips. He kissed it gently, and my heart did that little fluttery thing in my chest.

Oh, my.

I never expected Pacey Ziglar.

And every time he did something like this? He surprised me more.

Hunter just walked away, he and his little cronies talking to one another about something or other. I couldn't care less what they were doing, but I hated that I allowed him to take up so much headspace.

"You're going to come over later to study after your lunch, right?" Pacey asked as we made our way to the parking lot.

"That's the plan. I want to get through those notes while they're still fresh in my mind. But also, I think my head hurts too much right now to go over it."

"You have that late lunch with the girls anyway, as you said. You don't want to miss that."

I smiled. "I don't. Even though I do, and I'm kind of nauseous thinking about it. They are my friends. I need to get over whatever the hell's wrong with me."

Pacey frowned as he walked me to my car. "There's nothing wrong with you."

"Well, you can't convince me of that at this moment."

"I could try," he said, his voice a purr.

Oh, he *could* try. And he'd probably be very good at it, but I wouldn't allow that to happen. Not yet. Because I needed to focus on driving without swooning.

And I did not swoon.

Pacey leaned down and brushed his lips against mine. "Drive safe. Text me when you get there."

I rolled my eyes. "I think I'll be okay. I have done this driving thing a few hundred times."

"Let me be a mother hen."

I warmed inside again, and then told myself to put on the brakes.

There was no use getting all warm and romantic about him. We were only enjoying each other. We didn't need to get too into anything more.

He reached around, slid his hand down to the small of my back, and pressed me closer to him. I moaned and nearly wrapped my arms around him so I could climb him like a tree.

Someone honked, and we pulled back from each other, the moment shattered.

"Whore," Hunter called as he drove off, speeding out of the parking lot in his sports car, even though it was the middle of winter in Colorado.

"Idiot," I growled.

"For more reasons than one."

Pacey searched my face. "Are you okay?"

"About his words? Of course, I am. I'm not a whore. Even if I slept with a different guy every night, as long as it was safe and consensual, I wouldn't be a fucking whore. He just doesn't have the vocabulary to say anything else. And he's Sanders' friend, who probably knew that Sanders was cheating on me the entire time. And he didn't care. To him, women can be one of two things: whores or moms. And, occasionally, they can switch off. As I am neither, I don't need to exist for him, other than as someone to push down."

"I love your mind sometimes," Pacey said, shaking his head, though there was a smile on his face.

"I just hate that I've been spending so much time worrying about him. Or at least thinking about him."

"So, let's not let that happen." He pressed a quick kiss to my lips. "Call me when you get there. Or I'll text Nessa to annoy you for the rest of the evening."

"Thank you for that, because I have a feeling you're going to anyway, and she'll jokingly razz me the whole evening."

"That's our Nessa."

That warmed me. I wasn't jealous that he had female friends. Far from it. I liked that we were all close in our own ways. "I love that you guys are best friends."

"Me, too. Though I haven't been spending as much time with her lately." He winced. "I need to do better about that."

"Is she coming over to study tonight?"

"No, she has a group project again, but I'm going to figure something out. You're okay if I hang out with her by myself? That's not an issue?"

I shook my head, surprised that he even asked. "You're not Sanders. We've gone over this."

"Good, but I still wanted to double-check. She's my friend, and I want to make sure that I don't ignore her for other parts of my life."

"That makes you an excellent friend," I said softly. "Okay, we've been standing out here long enough that I'm cold."

"I'd offer to warm you up, but sadly, I don't think that's in the plans."

"Sorry," I teased. "How about you text me when you get home?" I said with a laugh.

"Touché."

I waved as I walked away, shaking my head.

I didn't have a problem with Pacey and Nessa being friends. I hadn't had a problem when Corinne was their friend, either. The three musketeers had been close before I came along. They had grown closer in the short period of time after Elise and Dillon started dating, but they had been together for a while. At least, through college.

I wouldn't stand in the way of that, even though I knew some other girls might. Pacey just didn't cheat. Sometimes, he gave too much of himself, but I didn't think that was on anyone else.

I shook my head, pushing those weird thoughts away.

No need to worry about something that I hadn't been concerned about before.

I drove towards the house and parked in the back, grateful that I didn't have to park on the street.

I pulled out my phone as I turned off the car.

Me: *Just pulled in. I'm safe.*

Pacey: *Good. I was about to send out the calvary.*

Me: *I take it Nessa's home?*

Pacey: *You've got it. See you tonight.*

I made my way inside, shucked off my coat and boots, and went to put my things away. We wouldn't be studying during lunch, although I probably should. However, this afternoon was about roommates and getting to know one another better. The other girls were already in the kitchen as I made my way inside. I smiled.

"You're here," Natalie said as she gave me a one-armed hug. "We went with the typical trendy cheeseboard," she said. "I don't know if we can call it a true charcuterie because we don't have the right meat to cheese ratio, but we did add tons of veggies and fruit as we have to be healthy."

"I'm so glad that adult Lunchables are on trend," I said, my mouth watering.

"Same," Nessa said, her eyes bright. "How was class?" she asked.

"I figured Pacey would have told you," I said with a laugh.

She frowned and shook her head. "He just said to make sure you got home safe. Class sucked, then?"

I nodded. "Pretty much. I'm just really hoping that I don't end up with this guy as my advisor for my thesis."

"That would be horrible, from what I remember you

saying," Elise said as she set out four glasses. "I made peach iced tea. I realize it's winter, but I was craving it, and I made too much. I hope that's okay."

"That sounds wonderful." I looked around. "Is there anything I can do? I'm sorry that I was late."

"You had the latest class. It's not your fault," Natalie said and squeezed my hand. "Now come on, I'm starving."

"Here, help me carry the plates," Nessa said as she handed me some.

I smiled and took the stack from her. "That, I can do. And I'll do whatever dishes are left."

"Deal," all three women said at the same time. I laughed.

We sat around the coffee table, each of us sitting on the floor. There were tons of chairs in the room, but this seemed a little more intimate and fun.

Almost like a slumber party without the slumbering.

"When do you have your next appointment?" Natalie asked as she slid some brie onto a cracker.

"On Monday. And then another on Wednesday. And two on Thursday. All of this while dealing with exams. It's a lot, but I'm going to get it done."

"And the whole boyfriend thing probably isn't helping," Elise added, her eyes twinkling.

"I wouldn't call Pacey my boyfriend," I said quickly.

"He's not?" Nessa asked.

I winced. "We haven't exactly had that conversation."

"What kind of conversation *have* you had?" Elise asked.

"The one where we told each other that we are exclusive and are getting to know one another. That our labels are the fact that we are exclusive, not what other labels we haven't given ourselves yet."

"That's better than what most people begin with."

I nodded at Elise.

"Oh," Nessa said after a moment, "I just thought...I don't know. You guys seemed to get serious pretty quickly."

I frowned, studying Nessa's face. "I mean, we're as serious as sex can be because I'm not going to shy away from that," I answered, even though I knew I was blushing. "But we're in college, and he doesn't even know if he's going to stay in the country after we graduate." I ignored the odd twinge I felt at that statement. "And I just got out of a very long, practically *lifelong* relationship. I can't even think the word *serious*. But I can have fun." My voice got a little more high-pitched towards the end, and I realized I was speaking far too fast even as I kept going. The girls shared a look before smiling at me.

"Don't worry, we're not grilling you. Sorry," Elise said. "We won't bring it up again."

"Yeah, let's not," Nessa said before piling things on her plate. I frowned, trying to figure out what I was missing.

And then I looked at the grimace on her face, saw how she had been acting over the past few weeks, and it hit me.

I was such a fucking idiot.

"What's wrong?" Natalie asked? "Did we make you sad?"

For a moment, I thought she was talking to Nessa, but no, it was directed at me.

Apparently, I wasn't good about hiding my emotions.

Instead of answering, I just smiled. "I'm okay. It's just the whole: 'Oh my God, it's a boy, what do I do?' thing. Typical college stuff. Now, let's talk about all of you. Because I am *over* talking about myself."

Nessa smiled as she looked at me, but did it reach her eyes? Had I made another mistake?

How long has Nessa been in love with Pacey?

And why am I only figuring it out now?

"You know, the last time we did something like this, Corinne spiked all of our iced tea," Elise said, her eyes a little watery but a smile on her face.

"Oh, yes, with vodka. But it was the good vodka that we got from one of our other friends," Natalie continued. "You couldn't even taste it."

"I think I ended up dancing in my bra on the coffee table," Nessa added and winced. "I'm happy that we were able to fix the hole in that wall," she said, and I looked between the three of them, nodding as they talked about Corinne and shared different stories about a house I had never lived in.

They weren't pushing me out, they were talking with me, and I smiled and added on to the small stories I knew about her.

But Corinne wasn't with us anymore.

And I wasn't sure what any of us were supposed to do about it.

I missed her, too. But I wasn't her.

And every time they told these stories about the vivacious Corinne with her heart of gold and a smile that could make anybody have a better day, I realized how much I lacked.

And I hated myself just a little bit more.

I looked at Nessa again as she gave me a curious look, and then I quickly stuffed a grape into my mouth and smiled.

Natalie and Elise kept speaking, discussing a party or some other thing, and Nessa just looked at me before quickly glancing away with an expression on her face that I couldn't read.

Did she hate me?

How much had I already taken from her?

One of her best friend's rooms?

And now the boy she loved.

I needed to talk to Pacey. Soon.

Because I was an idiot.

And I had a feeling that he was even more oblivious.

THIRTEEN

Pacey

IT WAS NEVER GOOD TO GET A TEXT SAYING THAT someone needed to talk. It was also never good to have it come from a girl who you weren't sure was your girlfriend but was close enough. Hell, I wasn't even sure we were far enough into our relationship to have a we-need-to-talk talk, and yet, here we were.

The guys were all out, Tanner on a date with his pair, and Miles on a study date. Dillon had just left for work, and I knew Elise would meet him at the brewery. I wasn't quite sure how the two made working at a bar their date, but it worked, and I was glad for them.

Maybe once I wasn't working as many hours as I was on extra labs, and my health was a little bit better, considering this cough just wouldn't go away, I'd see if Dillon needed an extra pair of hands at the bar. I wanted to work, to do something, and not solely rely on trust funds.

Plus, I liked the place—the vibe of it.

And now, I was thinking about working and bars rather than the fact that Mackenzie was coming over, and I had no idea what she wanted to talk about.

The doorbell rang, and I tried not to run to it. Mostly so I didn't appear too eager, but also because my lungs weren't up to it. I was pretty sure I had another infection that was slowly seeping down my nasal passages, but I was fine.

I shouldn't have kissed Mackenzie that morning because I didn't want to get her sick, and that was on me.

Jesus, I needed to do better.

But it wasn't like this cough had been there this morning. It had shown up suddenly and was now scaring the crap out of me.

I shook that away and opened the door.

Mackenzie was there, a bright smile on her face that was kind of terrifying. Mostly because it didn't reach her eyes and had a bit of a manic quality to it.

"Mackenzie?"

"Hey."

"Hey," I said softly.

"Why are you so pale? Is everything okay?"

"I was about to ask what's wrong with you, but let's get you inside since it's winter and you don't need to catch a cold."

And I didn't need to give one to her.

She already had enough on her plate without dealing with my issues or getting sick.

She walked in, gave me a weird look, and I leaned down

to kiss the top of her head. "I'm feeling a little under the weather," I said honestly. "I don't want you to get sick," I added.

Her eyes widened. "Pacey, do you need me to leave? Wait, I have to say something first, and then I'll leave."

"That's not foreboding at all," I said softly.

She winced. "Go sit on the couch."

"I'm not an invalid," I grumbled.

"If you're feeling under the weather to the point that you can't kiss me? Go sit down. I'll wrap you in a blanket. And if you're not careful, I'll microwave you some tea and make you some soup."

I visibly shuddered. "Don't even joke about that."

"What, you don't like my soup?"

"Ha ha," I replied. I sat down on the couch and let Mackenzie wrap me up in a blanket. She sat on the other end of the sofa and looked at me.

"Talk to me. What's wrong?"

"I don't know how to begin this."

"Now you're scaring me."

She swallowed hard. "Seriously, I think we fucked up."

My eyes widened. "How?"

"I'm just going to start at the beginning. Tell you about everything that's been going on, and see if I can get it out. Because maybe I'm wrong and I can talk my way through it."

"Now you're worrying me," I said but sat back as she spoke.

"So, I went over to talk cheese and everything," she began, and I blinked.

"Cheese?"

She waved her hand. "We had a cheeseboard. We couldn't call it charcuterie because of the amount of meat involved," she said, and I snorted. I couldn't help it. She rolled her eyes. "Yes, a penis joke. Hilarious. I'm having an existential crisis right now. Can you let me continue?"

I nodded and looked at her. "Of course. Talk to me."

"It's just...it's weird, I feel like a replacement there. That's not why I'm here, but it began it all."

"You're not a replacement."

She shook her head. "I know that, but it's how I feel. They have all these amazing stories about Corinne, and she deserves to be spoken about. She deserves everything. It's not fair that she's gone, and we're all still learning to grieve and deal with it. But when they start talking about her, I have nothing to contribute. I only knew her for a couple of months. And now I'm in her room, living with her friends, and I'm not her." She looked up at me then. "I'm with you, and I feel like I'm taking her place there, as well."

My brows shot up. "Corinne and me? We were never like that. I promise. You're not taking her space anywhere, especially not with me." She opened her mouth to speak, and I shook my head. "Corinne was one of my best friends. We met at the beginning of the school year, thanks to a class we took, and we meshed. Corinne, me, and Nessa were just good friends. I'll hate every day that Corinne isn't here to see what happens with the rest of the world, and I hate that she's not going to graduate or thrive in her career. I hate that she won't find someone to marry. I hate that she's not going to have the family she wanted. But that doesn't mean I'm replacing her in my life with you. Your friends aren't doing it either."

She looked at me then and wiped away a tear. I wanted to pull her close, hold her, kiss her and tell her that everything would be okay. But in case I was sick with something contagious, I didn't. I just leaned back and stared at her, willing her to understand that she meant something to me.

"I'm glad that we all talk about her because she deserves so much more than what she got in the end. And it's on me that I feel like some weird replacement, but then again, sometimes I feel that...well, I shouldn't say it," she said and shook her head.

I frowned. "Just tell me. You're my friend, too. And something more. We both know that."

I hadn't meant to say that last bit, but she looked at me and swallowed hard. "I think that might be part of the problem."

I froze, something inside me twisting. "What's part of the problem? What are you talking about?"

"As I said before, I think we messed up."

"How did we do that?"

"Pacey, this might not be my place, but I think it needs to be—"

"Just spit it out," I growled, annoyed with myself more than her.

She pressed her lips together and nodded. "I think Nessa's in love with you," she whispered.

My eyes widened, and I nearly laughed. "No, she isn't," I said, and Mackenzie winced.

"I think she is," she murmured.

"No, she isn't. She's my friend. There may be a kind of love there with the friendship, but it's nothing more than that. We're not like that."

She shook her head. "I kept ignoring the way she looked at you because I thought it was just friendship. Maybe I didn't want to see you differently either. But she's changed since you and I slept together. Now that we're spending so much time together."

"Changed how?" I asked, my voice cool. I needed it to be. I couldn't think, couldn't focus. Because Mackenzie had to be wrong.

"Nessa's been a bit cold around me, a little more distant. And even sometimes far too bright, as if she's hurting inside. And it's all my fault. I thought it was because I had stepped into Corinne's shoes at the house, but I don't think it's that. I believe it's something more. I think I screwed up. There's a code. You're not supposed to be with the guy your friend crushes on. And yet, I'm doing that." She looked at me then, her eyes pleading. I wanted to ignore her, wanted to walk away. "I really think Nessa's in love with you, Pacey."

I blinked, trying to catch up, my breathing now labored —though I didn't think that part was from the news.

I snorted, trying to laugh. "You're wrong. There's no way she loves me. We're mates, she and I. That's it. I know some people don't understand that you can be friends with a girl, but you can, and I am."

She shook her head. "Guys and girls can be friends. And I believe that on your end, it's only friendship," she said quickly.

"You're damn right, it is," I growled.

She pulled back, and I wanted to curse. "Mackenzie," I began.

She shook her head. "Maybe I'm wrong. I hope I am, but I see the way she looks at you now that I'm letting myself see. I notice how she tries not to. And I can feel how she's starting to hate me because I swooped in and took you away out of nowhere."

"You're wrong," I growled. "She was never meant to be mine. She isn't mine. She's my friend. Don't twist this," I said, scared now.

She reached out, gripped my knee, and swallowed hard. "Maybe I'm wrong. I want to be wrong. Maybe I'm just having one of those times where I read too much into everything. And that's on me. I'm sorry if I ruined things between you and Nessa or between us or made things difficult. But I need you to know this. I'm so sorry. All of this is on me. If something changes between you and Nessa, it's all my fault. I would understand if you never wanted to see me again. If you pushed me away and we never talked, it would be my fault. But I wanted you to know what I saw. Because what if I'm right? What if we're hurting her by being together?"

I swallowed hard and leaned back against the cushions. "I don't want to talk about this," I said, worried now. I needed to think, had to go over my every interaction with her.

And I was so afraid that Mackenzie was right.

Because I was blind. And, fuck, what if I was hurting Nessa?

"Okay, we can talk about something else. We can talk about school, or I can go. I'm sorry. I probably shouldn't have said anything, but I really don't want to hurt Nessa. She's my friend. What if we're hurting our friend?"

"I get what you're saying and why, and I'll think about it later, but I can't talk about it right now. Jesus, Mackenzie. What if you're right?"

Her eyes filled with tears, but she blinked them away quickly. "Exactly. What if I'm right? I don't know what I'll do. We need to fix this. She's our friend," she whispered.

"You're right. She is. And, Jesus, I hope to hell you're wrong."

"Me, too. It'd be great if I had overreacted and wasn't adding something else to our already strenuous piles."

"Why does this all have to be so damn hard?" I growled out.

"Because we're complex, and we have a lot of friends. And, sometimes, we fuck up."

She sighed. "Or maybe I'm just overreacting. I want to be overreacting."

She let out a breath and ran her hands through her hair. It made her look all tousled and sexy, and if I weren't afraid that I would lose my breath just looking at her, I would lean forward and take her. Anything to get my mind off Nessa and the fact that I could be hurting her.

"So, what else is going on?" she asked.

"Let's see, school, friends, lack of work, though I am thinking about asking if I can work with Dillon once I have time."

Her eyes widened. "You'd be good behind the bar."

I snorted. "You know, the accent could help with tips."

"Damn right, it would," she said, teasing. She was smiling, though it didn't quite reach her eyes. We were both on a precipice, stressed out. But we'd figure this out. We had to.

"Anything else? Oh, how was dinner with your dad?"

I gritted my teeth. "I didn't tell you, did I?" I asked.

Her eyes widened. "What do you mean? What

happened? I assumed everything went all right because you didn't say anything."

I let out a breath. "My father brought his girlfriend to dinner."

She blinked at me, staring. "Your dad has a girlfriend?" she asked.

I let out a growl.

"A *pregnant* girlfriend," I quipped.

"No," she said, and I nodded.

"Yep. And now we know the reason my parents' marriage, the one that was so strong for over twenty years, blew up. Because my dad is a fucking nob and can't keep it in his pants."

"Pacey, I'm so sorry."

I shook my head, my chest tightening. Hopefully, it was just stress, because Jesus, it was hard to breathe. "I'm fine," I replied and shook my head again. "I think. They tried to explain it to me, say that they were in love and that things changed or whatever the fuck. I don't bloody know. My dad has a girlfriend who's not much older than me, and she's pregnant." I paused. "Fuck, I'm going to have a baby sister or brother."

"Pacey," Mackenzie whispered.

"Hell, this is all a little too fucking much. I cannot believe they did this. My parents loved each other. They went through so much shit with me when I was a kid," I said and then closed my mouth.

"What do you mean?"

"Just, you know, normal stuff," I said. I didn't know why I was lying. I shouldn't. It wasn't like my disease was a secret. I just didn't talk about it.

I rubbed my chest, my breathing coming a little harder. Hell, maybe I *was* sick.

"Anyway, my parents? They were the epitome of love and happiness. And my dad threw it all away."

"I'm so sorry, Pace."

I smiled softly. "You called me Pace."

"Oh, I didn't mean to. Do you not like it?"

"I do. I always wanted to call you Mac, but now that I know Hunter calls you that, I don't want to anymore."

She grimaced. "He did kind of ruin that name for me."

"Then you'll always be Mackenzie to me." I coughed, blinked. "Shit," I growled.

She moved to her knees and then leaned forward. "Pacey? What's wrong?"

"I'm fine," I rasped before I started coughing again. And I kept coughing.

My shoulders shook, and my lungs rattled, and still, I kept coughing.

Mackenzie's eyes widened, and she leaned forward more, saying something to me. But I could barely hear it. I couldn't hear anything.

I kept hacking, and it became harder and harder to breathe. Mackenzie reached for me, and then there was nothing.

FOURTEEN

Mackenzie

MY CHEST HURT, AND I DIDN'T KNOW IF THE labored breathing came from a possible sickness or the fact that I had almost watched Pacey die.

This couldn't be happening. Pacey had to be okay.

I paced the hospital waiting room, expecting someone to show up that wasn't just me, but I was alone. I'd had to call 911 for the first time in my life, and the paramedics had come and whisked Pacey away in an ambulance. An actual ambulance. I had even ridden with him. I had thought maybe I should drive and follow so I'd have my car, but my hands were shaking so much, they had asked if I wanted to ride along, so I had.

I'd never been in an ambulance before, and I never wanted to be again.

I would never get the image of Pacey looking at me before succumbing to a coughing fit and passing out in my arms out of my head.

I had reached out to him and caught him before he fell off the couch and hit his head on the coffee table. He would have smacked his face right on the corner and probably would have gotten hurt far worse than he already was.

I wish I'd been quicker. Wished I had done something. Pacey had mentioned he thought he might be sick but said that he just needed some rest. So, we had sat there and talked. And what had I done? I had added more worries to his plate by talking about Nessa.

I shouldn't have. "This is all my fault," I berated myself. He was in the hospital, and there was nothing I could do.

And nobody else was here. I had called Elise to tell her what had happened, and she had said that she would rally the troops so people knew what was going on.

I couldn't even go back to be with him because I wasn't family, nor did I have his family's information. I had taken his phone, but I didn't know his access code, so I couldn't find his emergency contact information—if he even had it in there. But the nurses said that they could handle all of that since they were going to do what they could. But it wasn't like they could tell me anything. I was glad that they couldn't because it meant they followed the HIPAA rules, but I wanted them to tell me *something*. I needed to know how Pacey was. I didn't even know where he was in the hospital anymore. They couldn't say anything to me. I felt so alone, wondering if Pacey would be okay.

"Mackenzie Thomas?" I looked up to find a nurse in soft pink scrubs, a small smile on her face.

"That's me." I practically tripped over my feet to get to her.

She held out her hand, keeping me steady. "It's okay. Mr. Ziglar is in the back. He's asking for you."

"He's awake?"

Her eyes were kind as she smiled. "Yes. Come on back. He asked for you specifically, so you're welcome to follow me. You can't stay for long because he needs his rest, but I'm sure he will be happy to see you."

"Okay, okay. I know you can't tell me anything, but if he's awake, then *he* can tell me." I let out a breath, telling myself to calm down. "I'm babbling, and I feel like I'm going to have a panic attack, and I've never really had one before."

She paused and looked at me. "Deep breaths. We can get you some water if you think that will help. Okay?"

I swallowed hard. "I can do that. I think."

"Good girl. We'll get you some water. You sit down right next to your man over here and take care of each other. It's been a long night already, and he's going to need to stay overnight."

Fear twisted inside me, and I nodded. "Okay. Just tell me what to do."

"Sit. We'll take care of you both." I stood in front of an open doorway, but I couldn't see who was in the bed. I froze. "Go inside. He's waiting."

I looked at her then, and she smiled kindly again. I propelled myself forward.

Pacey lay in the bed, his usual debonair attitude a little softer, his face pale, his hair disheveled. He had an IV in his arm but a small smile on his face. He also had oxygen going into his nostrils, and it scared me.

"Pacey," I whispered.

He smiled again and held out a hand. "Come on over here, though you should probably wash your hands first before the nurses yell at us."

I nodded, looked at the sink, then correctly scrubbed my hands, noticing that they were shaking. I added hand sanitizer after I dried them and then wordlessly walked over to the side of the bed. "Sit, Mackenzie. I'm okay."

A single tear fell, and I swallowed hard, trying to catch my breath.

"You say that, and yet I don't know if I believe you."

"Mackenzie," he whispered and held out his hand.

I slid mine into his as I sat, trying to breathe. "What's wrong?"

"A lot of things. But nothing," he said, and I frowned.

"That's the worst non-answer ever."

"True," he said before letting out a breath. "First, I need you to know I'm going to be fine."

The nurse walked in at that moment and handed me a paper cup full of water.

"When you're done, I can show you where the guest lounge is and some other things, but I'll let you finish talking. You keep resting, Mr. Ziglar."

"Call me Pacey," he said, and she rolled her eyes.

"Don't think that little smile and accent will get you out of resting."

She shook her head and then walked away, and Pacey just smiled wider. "They like taking care of me. They're good at their jobs here."

"You say that as if you've been here before," I said slowly, trying to catch up. What's going on?" I asked, swallowing hard after I took a sip of water.

He sighed and patted my hand. "I'm okay. I promise. This is something I've had to deal with for a while."

I wanted to shake him so he'd open up and tell me more, but I knew that would only hurt him and not help anything. "Okay, but how? Why don't I know this?"

"Because it's all a bit embarrassing, and I don't talk about it. In my family, we don't talk about illness." He frowned. "We don't talk about a lot of things, actually, but I digress."

"Pace," I said.

"When I was eight, I had a kidney transplant," Pacey began, and my eyes widened.

"Pacey," I said, not having expected to hear that at all.

"The fact that I made it to eight without needing one was a miracle. When I was born, my right kidney decided to stop working. It gradually dropped to fifty percent capacity and slowly worked its way down to barely three percent. When it got below that, it started to secrete other hormones that hurt my body and increased my blood pressure to the point where I was in and out of hospitals until I was eight. When I was two, they removed that kidney. However, my left one began to overcompensate and was working too hard for my body."

"Oh," I whispered, not knowing what else to say.

He smiled softly. "I had the best doctors. And who knows, if it had happened now, maybe I could've saved both kidneys. Medicine has changed a lot in the past twenty years." He let out a breath as I just sat there, staring at him, squeezing his hand for dear life. "When I was seven, my left kidney finally decided it'd had enough. I was on dialysis for a year until they found a kidney that was a perfect match for me. So, I only have one working kidney, and it isn't even the one I was born with. But I still call it mine."

I sat there, trying to breathe, attempting to catch up. He'd been through so much and had never mentioned it. We might be new in terms of a relationship, but I knew that he hadn't told anyone else this story either. He'd kept so much to himself, held his secrets tightly to his chest for so long. "So, all of this is from your kidney?"

"Not precisely," he said softly. "Thanks to the kidney transplant, I got a lovely, long-term autoimmune disease. Something that's chronic and recurrent. It happens in only a small percentage of people, but I guess I was lucky. It's called hypogammaglobulinemia."

"How do you even spell that?" I asked, blinking.

Pacey smiled. "It took a while, but I learned. Anyway, because of it, I get infections pretty easily. Bronchitis or ear infections mostly, sinus infections. Sometimes even skin infections. We're cautious with it because it can lead to organ damage and other things if left untreated, but if I knock on wood right now, I'm doing okay."

"Pacey, I can't even imagine. And you've been dealing with all of this alone?"

He shook his head. "I have my family," he whispered. "Despite the hell we're going through now, I know if I were to call them, they would be here immediately."

"That's a good thing then, right? That they're always here for you?"

"Yes, it's a good thing. I thought the fact that they stayed together during all of my bad days meant they could outlast everything. But I was wrong," he whispered, shrugging.

"Pacey," I whispered.

"No, it's fine, I promise. I just need to deal with it, and I haven't been dealing with it quite well enough."

"I'm so sorry. So, what does this all mean?"

"It means that I get colds easily, and sometimes if I'm not careful, I can get pneumonia. I'm not there yet, but I passed out because I wasn't getting enough oxygen, and I haven't been taking care of myself. I'm usually better at it, but it's been a weird few months. I didn't have any symptoms for nearly a year, but stress can induce it."

My eyes widened. "Corinne," I whispered.

"Yes. Once I get my new meds, and everything settles down, a lot of times it's like nothing's wrong. I have to be careful about some of the vaccines that I get and over-the-counter medications I use, but I just have to be aware. And, usually, I am. It's why I don't drink heavily. I always want to make sure that I'm in as much control and as aware as possible."

"I'm so sorry, Pacey."

"It's okay. You got me the help I needed."

"Good, I'm glad I could help."

"Thank you for being there. I would have been alone, you know, if you hadn't."

I wiped away tears, even as he smiled softly. "I'm the one who added more stress to your system. You might not have even passed out if I hadn't."

He shook his head. "I was having trouble breathing

before you even showed up. I would have been alone, Mackenzie. But I wasn't because of you. So, thank you." He squeezed my hand again.

"Well, now that I know, it means I'm going to have to scrub your house from top to bottom. I'm just saying. We are not going to let you get sick again."

He snorted and smiled at me. "Trust you to make a plan."

"You haven't even begun to see my plan. There will be color-coded charts to make sure you're at peak performance." I paused. "And you're going to have to tell your roommates. They need to know that if they even get a hint of the sniffles, they need to stay away from you."

"You're right. I do need to tell them."

My phone buzzed, as did his. I pulled both out of my purse. "Oh, I had your phone," I said, blushing, and handed it over.

"It seems we're on the same group text."

"They're all outside. I should let you get some rest," I said after a moment. "I can let everyone know how you're doing. At least, the basics."

"I'll explain everything to them tomorrow when I get home. If you can just tell them that I have a little bit of a cough, that'd be great."

"They're going to have a lot of questions," I said, giving him a pointed look.

"About my illness? Or the fact that you're here with me right now?"

"Probably both. After all, I don't think they know what we're doing."

"*I* don't know what we're doing," I whispered.

"Well, we're going to have to figure that out, too. But maybe after I'm out of the hospital," he said dryly.

"I would lean over and kiss you, but you know, you're indisposed and all."

"I can imagine it. This will be a long night."

"Are you going to call your parents?"

"I am. They need to know, and I want them to know. I just hope to hell my dad doesn't bring his girlfriend when he shows up."

"I guess maybe it's good that visiting hours are almost over," I whispered.

His eyes brightened. "Look at you, helping me out. I'm okay, love. I promise."

"I won't believe that until you're safely at home and I can tuck you in. And kiss you." I hadn't meant to say that, but his eyes warmed, and I swallowed hard.

I had no idea what the two of us were doing. I wasn't good at this, and I wasn't sure I would ever be good at it.

This was only supposed to be for fun. It wasn't supposed to turn serious. But here we were, sharing secrets. Sharing everything. I didn't know what I would have done if something worse had happened to Pacey. How had these feelings developed so quickly?

I squeezed his hand, said my goodbyes, and walked out to the waiting room.

He was only supposed to be my rebound. I wasn't supposed to fall for him.

One didn't fall for a rebound. That was an unspoken rule.

At least, that's what I told myself.

"Mackenzie," Nessa said as she ran towards me. "What happened?" She squeezed my hands, her eyes wild. "Talk to us."

"He has a cold or something. His lungs needed more air, and he passed out." I explained about the ambulance ride but didn't give them details. That would be up to Pacey.

"Can we see him?"

The nurse who had walked me in shook her head. I hadn't realized she was right behind me. "Unfortunately, visiting hours are over, but you can come back tomorrow. Although he should be out by then, so you can all go home."

I didn't miss the look Nessa gave me or the disappointment on her face.

We would have to talk because I didn't want to lose my friend, nor did I want Pacey to lose her.

"Did you drive here?" Tanner asked, his gaze on mine. I shook my head. "No, I rode in the ambulance."

"Well, most of us drove in separately since we were all in different places. I can give you a ride home."

I looked at the others and nodded. "My stuff's still at your place."

"We can pick it up. We've got you. Come on. It's been a long day."

I swallowed hard, hugged everyone—including Nessa—on my way out, and made my way to Tanner's car.

"She'll be okay," Tanner spoke after a moment of silence. I looked up at him as I slid into the car.

"What?"

"Nessa. It's just a crush. She thinks it's love, but it's just a crush."

"We shouldn't be talking about this," I muttered. I was already uneasy, and this wasn't helping.

"Well, someone needs to say it. Us all pretending it's not a thing will only get someone hurt in the end."

"This isn't the time. I don't think my brain can handle much more."

He nodded. "I understand. But she'll be okay. She doesn't hate you."

"She doesn't?" I asked, my voice cracking.

"No, she doesn't even blame you."

"How do you know that?"

"I just do."

"That's not very helpful," I whispered.

"Probably not, but it's the truth. You'll figure it out."

"You sure are talkative tonight," I said snidely. Tanner rarely spoke to me—or anyone for that matter.

He shrugged as he pulled onto the highway. "I say what I have to. I like Pacey. And Nessa. And you." He shot me a look, and I lowered my head. "It's okay that we're all still figuring shit out."

"You say that, and yet I don't know what I'm doing."

"And that's fine," Tanner said. "You're allowed not to know yet. But Pacey's going to be okay. And so is Nessa. And so are you."

Before I could think about anything to say to that, my phone buzzed. I looked at it quickly, hoping it was Pacey.

But it was a number I didn't want to see.

Sanders: *We need to talk.*

I rolled my eyes and nearly growled.

"What's wrong?"

"Just Sanders, saying we should talk."

"You should ignore him."

My phone buzzed again.

Sanders: *It's important. I wouldn't text you if it weren't. I need to talk to you.*

Me: *Okay, when?*

"Damn it."

"What's wrong?" Tanner asked again.

"He's saying it's really important."

"As in an emergency, like you need to go over there right now?" he asked, a little anger in his voice.

"I don't know."

Sanders: *We can meet on Friday. During your open period? We need to meet.*

"Well, apparently, he wants to meet on Friday so it can't be that big of an emergency. But hell, I haven't talked to him since the whole blowjob thing," I growled.

"Oh, yes, the time my fist finally got to hit his face. It was nice."

I snorted, glaring at Tanner. "Nice?"

"I try."

I sighed. "I should just get this over with. One last hurrah of: 'Get the fuck away from me.'"

"That's my girl," he said, and I snorted.

Me: *Okay. Friday.*

Sanders: *See you then.*

I slid my phone back into my purse and pinched the bridge of my nose.

"Why do I feel like that was a horrible mistake?"

"Because it's Sanders. It was always going to be a horrible mistake."

"Ouch," I said.

"It's the truth."

My brain hurt, and all I wanted to do was sleep. But I couldn't because I couldn't stop thinking—about Sanders, annoyingly, though also about Pacey and everything else.

My life had gotten far too complicated for its own good, and I had no idea what I was supposed to do next.

FIFTEEN

Pacey

IT HAD BEEN A WEEK SINCE I'D GOTTEN HOME, AND I was finally at a hundred percent. That's how quickly I recovered when I took care of myself—something I needed to remember the next time I got sick.

Thankfully, my professors had been pretty good about exams and papers, and I was able to keep up with the notes and things thanks to friends—mostly Mackenzie. She had been a godsend. I had missed three days of classes, but she had taken such detailed notes, it was like I was there.

And it gave us an excuse to study more together. Not that I needed an excuse to spend time with Mackenzie these days. Something had changed when she sat next to my hospital bed. Maybe it'd even shifted in the ambulance, though I hadn't been conscious for most of that. But we were different. I didn't know what that meant, other than the fact that I was falling for her. And I shouldn't. She wasn't in a place to fall for anybody. We were still playing around, or at least that's what I told myself. We weren't supposed to be anything more than rebounds, friends who had sex and fun. And yet, it didn't feel like that. It felt like something more. I needed to remind myself that I couldn't want anything more from her than what we already had. It would be bad for both of us. Wouldn't it?

We were in my bedroom since Miles had another study group over. He had more study groups than the rest of us, but he needed to with his classes. There were a lot more group projects, and when they gathered, they tended to take over the living room. I didn't mind so much, and I knew the others didn't, either. We made do. And there was so much fucking space in this house that it wasn't a problem. It was the main reason I liked staying here, even if it came with its own set of complications that I wasn't ready to get into.

"Damn it," Mackenzie said as she stomped inside and tossed her phone on the bed next to me. I raised a brow.

"Everything going okay, love?" I asked and held back a wince at using the endearment. Thankfully, she didn't read much into the word, but I tried my best not to use it with her even though I used it casually with others. Not when things were getting oddly serious, especially when we hadn't expected them to.

"It's Sanders," she grumbled.

"What?" I asked, grinding my teeth together. I did not like to hear about Sanders. It didn't matter that they were no longer together. He had been a huge part of her life. And she was excellent about never mentioning him. Was she still hurt because of it? Maybe. That's why he and she had started together, after all, but I didn't like this jealousy I felt towards him. He was nothing, inconsequential, and yet, perhaps he was far more important than I cared to admit.

"What did he do?" I asked.

"He texted me when I was leaving the hospital with Tanner, saying that he needed to meet urgently. First, he said at the end of the week, then he texted again saying it was an emergency and it needed to be right away. Then he bailed, giving some excuse or another. I don't fucking know. But I'm exhausted from it, and now I have to meet him tomorrow for coffee because he needs to talk to me."

I scowled.

"You don't need to talk to him at all if you don't want to," I said sharply.

She gave me a look that spoke volumes. "Oh, I know. I also know that I haven't actually spoken to him for weeks, and I should probably do that and get it over with."

"Why?" I asked.

She sighed. "Because he was a huge part of my life, for *most* of my life. Our parents are still best friends."

"I don't know if I like hearing that," I said, and it wasn't until she raised a brow that I realized I had said it out loud.

"Not that I have an opinion."

"No, you're allowed an opinion. It's more the fact that I can't make them not hang out. They're friends, and I think my mom is finally getting it through her head that Sanders and I will never be together again. It's going to make for an awkward summer and holidays for them, but I don't care. I'm not going to be with Sanders ever again. My parents just have to get that through their heads."

"Have you told them about us?" I asked, wondering why I even asked.

She blinked. "Actually, yes," she said and then winced. "I talked about class, and I brought you up a few times because you're part of my life, and then it just kept going. My mom got the idea that I talk about you too much," she said and blushed.

I leaned forward and ran my finger down her cheek. "I like that," I whispered.

"Well, anyway," she said, but she kept biting her lip, "my parents know about you, but only that we've been hanging out. Because that's an awkward conversation that I'm not in the mood to get into."

"I figured that out," I said and cleared my throat. "My parents don't know about you. Mostly because I'm not talking to them much at all right now. I mean, I'm trying to talk to my mother and aunt," I added, "but Mum feels weird, and now I know why. I didn't want to throw a new relationship in her face."

Mackenzie's smile softened.

"You're a good guy, Pacey."

I shook my head. "Not all the time. Before you walked in, I was having this lovely little daydream about exactly how bad I could be." I crooned the words, and she blushed.

"I thought we were supposed to study," she whispered.

"Oh, we can study. I'm sure there are lots of things we can study."

She lifted her chin and laughed, shaking her head. "You're terrible, but I kind of like it." She let out a breath. "I just wanted to let you know that I do have coffee with Sanders scheduled for tomorrow. I didn't want you to think

I was going behind your back if anyone saw us. I want closure, if that's what he wants. Or to tell him to his face that he can fuck off if he wants to get back together."

I swallowed hard and nodded. "That works. Thanks for telling me. Seriously. I like that you feel comfortable letting me know."

"Of course, I would let you know," she said softly. "I'm not going to keep things from you, Pacey. We're friends. And friends don't lie to each other."

Friends. I liked being friends with her. I didn't know what the hell I was thinking wanting more. We shouldn't want more. And yet, I did.

I was losing my damn mind, and I needed to stop stressing. I needed to live in the moment, something I wasn't good at, even though people thought I was.

"Do you want me to go with you?" I asked, blurting out the words before I even realized I was doing it.

She smiled softly. "It's during your one o'clock class, or I'd say 'yes' in a heartbeat. Mostly because someone needs to hold me back from strangling him."

"You know, I kind of like that you've already thought about this."

"Of course, I did. Sanders was my friend and boyfriend since we were five, possibly before that if you count the cradle joke that I used to use all the time, annoyingly."

"Nothing was annoying about that," I countered.

"Maybe, but I still think it was, especially in retrospect. I don't know. I have to figure out how I feel, beyond the anger. Maybe it's disappointment? For wasting so much time?"

"Is it wasteful if you figured out who you were along the way?"

She blinked and smiled softly at me. "That's a beautiful thing to say. And I kind of like that idea, rather than me feeling like I wasted my entire life trying to build a future with a guy who was just a piece of shit."

"You know, maybe you and my mother should meet," I said dryly.

Mackenzie's eyes widened. "Oh, well, um..."

I laughed and shook my head. "Stop, I was only teasing. You're welcome to meet my parents, though I don't know if you really want to meet my dad. I thought he was a great guy. I was wrong. My mother, though, she's pretty fantastic."

"I love how you sound when you talk about her."

"I love her. I love my dad, too. Though I don't like him much right now," I said honestly.

"I don't blame you. It was kind of a jerk thing to do. Everything he's done has pretty much been a jerk thing these days."

"I don't know what's going on with him. Some mid-life crisis thing that's giving me a fucking headache. But we'll deal. We always do."

"You're right, you will. And now we don't have to keep talking about them."

I grinned. "Good, because I'd rather talk about what I was thinking about before you came in."

She blushed. "Pacey, I thought we were trying to catch you up."

"There are many things that we could catch up on," I

growled and reached for her, putting my hand over her hip. "So?" I whispered.

"That's your line? So?" she asked with a laugh and tapped the book in front of her. "We have homework."

"We already did it."

"It's not checked off on my list. I need completed check-boxes, Pacey. You know this."

"Well, there's a box I'd like to check," I said, then met her gaze. I blinked for a second before we both burst out laughing.

"I cannot believe you just said that."

"That is the worst joke I've ever said in my life."

"Please never call my vagina a box."

"What would you like me to call it?" I asked, leaning over her. Her eyes widened, her lips parting.

"What?" she asked, her voice breathy.

"If I can't call it your box, would you like me to call it your pussy? What about your cunt? What if I call it mine?"

And then I took her lips. She wrapped her arms around me, licking at my mouth.

I nibbled at her before I deepened the kiss, needing her taste.

I groaned, hovering over her. She spread her legs wider, and I rested against her heat, her thighs cradling me.

"You're so soft and warm," I whispered.

"And you work very, very hard," she teased.

"Well then, I guess we'll just have to do something about that."

I grinned and kissed her harder.

I slowly kissed my way along her neck to her collarbone,

gently working her shirt open. She had on a button-up blouse and only a bra underneath.

My brows lifted. "Don't you usually wear a tank top?"

"I liked the idea of the soft silk against my skin today."

I groaned, needing more of her.

"You are so fucking sexy," I whispered, kissing her again.

And I kept kissing her, needing more. I licked between her breasts, keeping her lacy bra on before moving to the top of her pants, nibbling on her leggings' waistband.

She laughed, and I pulled them down, bringing her panties with them. I shoved them off the bed and spread her legs.

"You're so fucking sexy," I whispered before I latched on to her clit and sucked. Her hips shot off the bed, but I kept sucking, licking, and nibbling at her swollen lips.

"You taste so sweet," I whispered, needing more. I teased, and I licked, and then I speared her with two fingers, wanting to watch her as she came on my hand. Her whole body shook, and she looked down at me, her eyes wide. Still, I needed more.

I kissed her again and looked at her as she came, and then I knelt back, stripping off my shirt. She pulled at my pants, and I grinned before I leaned back on the bed. She whipped off her bra, her breasts falling free in front of my face. And since they were there, and I needed them, I latched on to her nipple, kissing her harder and sucking. She groaned before she pulled away and shimmied down my body. She pulled off my pants, and my cock sprang free. I grinned.

"Oh?" I asked.

"Oh," she said before sliding a flavored condom over my dick. I grinned, and she began sucking. We both shook before she slid her mouth over my cock. I groaned, throwing my head back in ecstasy. She squeezed my base, swallowing as much as she could, her cheeks hollowing. I pushed into her, needing more as I touched the back of her throat. She hummed. She played with my balls with her free hand and bobbed her head, keeping a rhythm that would make me come too quickly. I tugged at her hair, pulling her up.

"I need to be in you."

She nodded, her tongue peeking out from between her lips. "Ready?"

I grinned. "I think that's my line."

She looked at me, then tangled her hands with mine as she slowly, ever so slowly, sank onto my cock.

I met her gaze, both of us shaking, and then she began to move. She rode me with abandon, and I let go of her hands so I could slide my palms up her hips and ribs to cup her breasts. Her mouth parted, and I played with her nipples, needing to touch her, needing to feel her.

This was perfection, aching perfection that told me that if I weren't careful, I would fall for the one person I shouldn't. Because she wasn't ready. She couldn't be. We had no future, and that was something I had to keep telling myself. Yet I knew that wasn't the case. Because I wanted more, needed more. I was falling in love with Mackenzie Thomas.

She leaned forward and kissed me softly. I groaned and moved my hands to tug at her hair, squeezing her tighter. I couldn't get enough of her. I needed her—needed her more than anything.

I choked back a growl as she kept moving, and I thrust into her.

I felt like I was falling for her, and yet I was afraid I'd already fallen.

Not because of this, not because of this moment, but because of everything.

And I couldn't. Not with so much up in the air, not when I knew she would leave when she needed to. Because the best thing in the world would be to watch Mackenzie fly, to watch her bloom into what she was meant to be.

I couldn't hold her back. I couldn't love her. Only I was afraid I already did.

When she came, I followed her, and then I held her close. Her sleepy smile told me more than I wanted to know.

She would have to walk away soon because she needed to discover who she was without somebody else. She had all but said that when she spoke of Sanders, and I needed to let her.

Only my arms wouldn't let her go. And I was afraid, so damn afraid that my heart wouldn't either.

Sixteen

Mackenzie

My head ached, but I would be okay. At least that's what I told myself. I loved my major and my classes, but sometimes it was all a little bit much, especially all at once. I could only really blame myself, though. I had been the one to add the extra class to complete my course load on time. Perhaps if the school hadn't changed one of the courses from a fall semester to a spring semester course, I wouldn't feel like I was scrambling. But there was nothing I could do about it now. I just needed to focus.

And maybe I could have one less set of credit hours my final semester, though I didn't think that would happen.

"Hey, Mac," Hunter said as he walked by.

I closed my eyes and counted to five, telling myself I couldn't beat somebody up just because they were annoying.

"Hunter," I said.

"Did you find a new advisor yet?" he asked, a grin on his face.

The math department wasn't that big, so of course, everybody knew that I was scrambling. I couldn't hide it from them, even though it wasn't any of their business.

"I have a meeting today. Everything's fine."

It was my last meeting before I was forced to go to the professor I didn't want to work with. It seemed nobody could fit me in, not with the time and budget constraints we were working with. And while I understood, I still hated Dr. Michaels. He had lied to me—flat out. I hadn't been making up the idea that he had accepted me. But there was nothing I could do about it now. It wasn't like I could force him to work with me. He just wanted Hunter and the Williams' family connections. It wasn't lost on me that Hunter's family contributed to the school. They donated a lot to the campus, so Hunter basically got to do whatever he wanted. And I got to pretend that I wasn't bitter about it. At least, in public. I could be upset when talking with the girls or Pacey.

They understood.

"Good luck. I'm sure you'll find something. Or you could switch to a major you'll actually succeed at. You don't have to keep trying at this."

I narrowed my eyes. "Thanks for the pep talk."

"I'm just trying to help."

"You're not. And I don't know what you have against me. We're not even going for the same things after school."

It honestly surprised me that he'd even stuck with the math major. For all Hunter's faults, and there were many of them, he was still a genius. I couldn't deny that. I couldn't even be jealous about it. Because he was just damn good at what he did. I *could* hate him for everything else that he did to me and in his life.

"I'm just saying, I don't know why you keep putting yourself in these situations," he said.

"I'm not doing anything, Hunter. Now I'm going to be late for my meeting. You should just go."

"Whatever," he said before walking away. I hated that this was the one class I had with Hunter that I didn't have with Pacey. And I hated that I was even thinking that. I had dealt with Hunter for nearly as long as I had been with Sanders. I could deal with him longer, even if I hated him.

He was just so annoying, and he seemed to love razzing me. He might be a genius, but he had never wanted for anything. Nor did he work toward anything. His version of studying was just knowing things. I could be jealous of that, but I didn't have the energy. I had work to do, and Hunter didn't get to take up any of my time by annoying the hell out of me.

I finally moved away and headed towards Dr. Jackson's office. I liked her, and I hoped she had a spot for me. I knew the money was tight, but hopefully, we could make it work. I knew not all schools were like this. Undergrads didn't always need an advisor or a final thesis or any of the stress I was dealing with. And if I had gone to another school, I probably wouldn't be in this situation. But I hadn't, and now I needed to deal with the consequences.

I knocked on Dr. Jackson's doorjamb since her door was open, and she smiled up at me and then waved me in. Although, I noticed the expression wasn't very bright.

Well, crap.

"Mackenzie, I'm glad to see you."

I took a seat, trying to keep *my* smile. "Hi. Thank you for taking the time to talk with me."

"I'm so sorry you're dealing with this," she said after a moment and then shook her head. "Dr. Michaels is brilliant. I thought you were going to work with him. Honestly, I was a little jealous at first."

Hope sprang eternal, and I leaned forward. "Things didn't work out. He decided to go with someone else so I'm still looking for an advisor."

She smiled again softly, and I knew the blow was coming. "I'm so sorry, Mackenzie. I know I could've done this via email, but I wanted to try to work something out with you."

I swallowed hard, tears pricking the backs of my eyes. "Oh?"

If she pushed me away, said she didn't have the money or time or space, I would have to work with Dr. Linde. The asshole professor who didn't like women, didn't like people in general, and was even worse than Dr. Michaels. I wasn't sure if I'd be able to deal with that.

"Mackenzie, I really can't. You were on my list, but when the time came, I was explicitly told that you'd be working with Dr. Michaels, so I picked someone else."

"You're working with Pacey," I blurted and shook my head. "Sorry."

"I thought you guys might be friends or something more," she said and shook her head. "It's none of my business. But, yes. Pacey and three others. I'm allowed one minor and three majors, with my budget and time. And, frankly, even that extra major is a little too much for me. But my family and I are making it work because I want to spend time with my kids." She shook her head. "I know Dr. Linde isn't working on the same program you want. He isn't exactly who you were looking for at all I'm sure, but I have a plan," she said, and my eyes widened, even as I tried to swallow back the disappointment.

"I like plans," I said cautiously. She gave me a small smile. "I've seen some of your schedules and spreadsheets over the past couple of years. I knew we could be friends."

"I like things color-coded with checkboxes."

"Same."

I hated that she wouldn't be my advisor. Though she hadn't been my first choice because her focus wasn't exactly what I wanted. Still, she would be better than Professor Linde. But now, I wasn't going to get her either.

"As I was saying, I thought I could try to co-chair your plan. I don't know how it'll work, and I don't want to get your hopes up too high, but maybe I can find a way. It's just that I wish it were with any other professor," she said and then pressed her lips together. "Not that I said that out loud. You didn't hear that from me."

I laughed, though there was no humor in it.

"Oh?"

"Yes, oh. I'm going to find a way to help you. I'm sorry I can't do it outright. I hate that you're in this mess. If you want to fight it, we can," she said quickly. "Dr. Michaels sent us emails, too, Mackenzie. We were all copied. We thought we had lost you to him."

I blinked, surprised, then swallowed the bile rising in my throat. "He did what?"

"He said you were taken. We all thought you would be a

perfect fit for him, at least in terms of what your focus wanted to be, so we looked elsewhere. We didn't know he would pick Mr. Williams at the last minute. I'm so sorry, Mackenzie. But we'll make this work. I promise. You're not going to flounder. We will make this work."

We spoke for a few minutes and got the beginning of the plan in order, but I couldn't breathe. I couldn't do much of anything.

Everything hurt, I was exhausted, and I didn't know what I was supposed to do next.

What was I supposed to do?

I said my goodbyes, but it was tough for me to imagine anything working. It couldn't, not when nothing was working out the way it should. How could this have happened? How could all of my plans just go awry?

I looked down at my phone and cursed at the notification. Of course, I couldn't just go home and wallow with ice cream and spreadsheets. No, I had to meet with my ex-boyfriend and see precisely what the hell he wanted.

My head hurt, and I just wanted everything to go away. And yet, I didn't have that option.

I sighed and made my way to the coffee shop. Sanders had said he would meet me on the third floor, and I had told Pacey where I would be, just in case something weird happened. Not that I thought it would, but I wanted others to know where I was anyway.

I had also told Natalie, just in case she was able to be around. Again, not that I thought I needed anyone as backup, but it was always smart.

I made my way towards the back area and didn't bother to get any coffee. I didn't want this to take long, and I didn't want him to think that I was suddenly okay with whatever would happen.

Sanders was in the chair, his head down, focused on his phone. I swallowed hard and rolled my shoulders back. I had told myself that today couldn't possibly get any worse, but I still had a meeting with my ex-boyfriend. It could get way worse. But I wouldn't allow it.

"Mac," he said, and I blinked. For some reason, it hadn't occurred to me that both he and Hunter called me Mac. I used to like it. It used to be a cute nickname. Pacey didn't want to use it because it hurt just a little because of Hunter, and it annoyed me that Sanders had taken something else from me.

And I hated myself—and probably him just a bit—for it.

"Sanders," I said before taking the seat across from him. He'd always been *Paul* to me growing up. Then, at the end of middle school, one of the cool kids he hung out with had called him "Sanders," and it had stuck. He hadn't wanted to be Paul because that could get you beaten up, at least according to that kid. So, he'd become Sanders, and I hadn't minded. It was just a name, after all, and it hadn't been my choice. I would've called him anything he wanted because I loved him. That's what you were supposed to do with people you loved.

I shook my head and pulled myself out of those thoughts. I needed to focus and stop acting like this.

"You wanted to meet?" I said, doing my best to keep my voice a bit cool. He had hurt me. I didn't want to be his friend. I didn't think he deserved even a fraction of that, but I also didn't need to be cruel. I only wanted to get this over with.

"I just have a few things to say. And I just...well, how are you?"

I shook my head. "I'm fine. You don't need to worry about me," I said.

"Oh. I'm glad that you're fine. It's good to hear that."

He started to ramble about something, and I just shook my head.

"Was there something you wanted? Because we're not together anymore, Paul," I said and cursed as he flinched at the use of the name. I used to call him both, and it hadn't been an issue. Now, it felt weird. I didn't need to be cruel. I just needed to be okay.

I needed to be okay with who I was and make sure that he knew I was done.

"I guess I just missed you."

I blinked. "Okay, good for you. But you don't need to tell me that."

Shit, I didn't know what to say.

"Why don't you tell me why I'm here?" I said, not too kindly.

"Hell, okay, Angela told me to come." I blinked.

"Angela?"

"My, uh...you know."

"Ah." The last girl I had seen him with. I didn't know her name, didn't need to know her name. That might be insensitive of me, but I didn't any part of that in my life anymore. I just wanted it gone. And he certainly wasn't making that any easier by bringing her up now.

"Anyway, Angela came to me, and...shit. She wanted me to apologize."

I blinked, wondering why he was telling me this. Why

did any of this matter? Why were we in public for him to tell me this? It shouldn't matter at all, and yet here he was, apologizing after all this time.

"What?" I bit out, my voice low.

"I don't know. I mean... After so many years, you and I were like the perfect thing, you know? We were amazing together, and I fucked it all up because I wanted to see what else was out there. And while I like Angela and all, she's not who I saw myself getting married to or anything. And my parents hate her, so I figured that you and I could maybe see if we could work things out. Or something. Because we shouldn't just throw everything away."

I blinked, my entire world crashing in around me. I couldn't be hearing this. Not after *months* of silence. After his cheating. Who the hell did he think he was? "You think I'll just forgive you and take you back after you *cheated* on me?"

He blushed. "I was kind of hoping you wouldn't make a scene."

I stood up, my chair tipping over. "You didn't want me to make a scene, so you asked me to forgive you for cheating on me while we were in a coffee shop? In public?" I asked, my voice low, but my body vibrating.

Everyone was staring now. We were in the quiet part of the coffee shop, but they were still looking.

"Shit. Stop acting like this. Maybe there's a reason I left you."

And there it was. The Paul who never took responsibility for anything. His parents had probably put him up to this. Oh, Angela might have told him to say that he was sorry, but his parents wanted us back together. Well, tough for them.

"No. Not even a little bit. I don't love you anymore, Paul. I don't even *like* you. Have fun with Angela. Have fun with the perfect little life you wanted because I'm not going to be a part of it. Oh, and maybe don't tell me it's a damn *emergency* when all you wanted to do was crawl back to me out of some kind of FOMO."

I turned on my heel and ran smack into Pacey. Could this day get any worse? Mortification slid through me as I looked up at him. "Did you hear that, by chance?"

"Oh, I did."

He looked over at Sanders. "This isn't over." And then he took my hand and pulled me out of the shop. People were still staring, but thankfully they were mostly looking at Sanders.

That piece of shit. I would feel sorry for him, but I didn't care enough.

"Oh my God," I whispered, my hands shaking as we stood outside where nobody could hear us.

"Mackenzie."

"I cannot believe he got me to come here for *that*." I put my hands on my face and resisted the urge to scream. I couldn't believe I had come here at all. For closure. Right. I was already closed. I was over him. Nothing about him mattered anymore. And yet, here I was, letting him into my thoughts again.

Pacey leaned forward and brought me close. "Do you want me to go back in there and hit him for you? I'm kind of jealous that Tanner got to do it, and I didn't."

That made me snort. "Sorry. I'm sad that I didn't get to deck him either. Damn Tanner and all the luck."

Pacey grinned down at me, and I ignored the little clutch I felt in my belly. It didn't mean anything. "We can hit him later." He kissed me softly, and I sighed, thoughts of Sanders and our past slowly fading away.

"Deal."

As Pacey kissed me again, I told myself this was just for now. Reminded myself that I didn't need to fall in love again. Falling in love hurt.

The next time the man I loved left me, it would break me.

So, I wouldn't fall.

I couldn't.

Seventeen

Pacey

MACKENZIE: *THIS EXAM IS HORRIBLE. WHY DID I need to take this class?*

Me: *Because it's a core credit, and you like the class.*

Mackenzie: *Stop making sense. And thank you again for coming to my rescue yesterday.*

I growled at that. If I had to think about that asshole, Sanders, again, I might have to murder someone. And I wasn't in the mood to go to jail.

Me: *Well, you and I are fine. And we never need to think about that wanker again.*

Mackenzie: *Deal. I need to go to class. But I'll talk to you soon?*

Me: *You can count on it.*

I put my phone away because I had almost said something silly like: *I love you*. I couldn't love Mackenzie. We were just hanging out. Having sex. Being friends.

I pinched the bridge of my nose and told myself that we weren't serious. We were only friends. And yet, I knew I needed to tell her something soon. Or I could simply hide my feelings and not worry about it. We were young, still figuring things out... I needed to stop focusing on what *could* happen and deal with what was right in front of me.

Nessa was coming over to study in the office, and Tanner and Miles were in their study area, focusing on whatever tests they had coming up.

Today was my first time being alone with Nessa since Mackenzie had mentioned her thoughts about how Nessa felt about me. I couldn't quite believe it. I mean, it was Nessa. We were friends. I thought we excelled at just being friends when people kept saying that we needed to be attracted to each other.

And yet, here I was, worried that maybe that was the case. Had I been wrong? Really bloody wrong?

I had to figure out what she was feeling or trust my gut instincts. Only I didn't think I could.

The doorbell rang, and I went to see who it was. Nessa stood on the other side, wringing her hands. Something was off, and I wasn't sure what to say.

Because I had a feeling I had fucked up. Big time.

"Hey," I said as I opened the door.

"Hey there," Nessa said and rocked back on her heels.

I let out a breath, then moved back. "Come on in. You don't want to catch a cold."

"Nor do we want *you* getting sick," she said. I gave her a

one-armed hug, and she squeezed back quickly before walking away.

Had she always done that? Or was it more so now?

Why was I messing up so badly so quickly all of a sudden? What was I doing wrong?

I had hoped that what Mackenzie had said about Nessa had just been her seeing things that weren't there, but I didn't think that was the case anymore. Now that I fought to remember every moment with Nessa, every look that I thought had been nothing...

Well, I wasn't sure what to do or feel about it.

I swallowed hard and tried to smile, but I wasn't sure what to say. Nessa gave me a weird look, and I smiled again. She rolled her eyes. "Are you okay?" And then she blinked. "Oh, no, is something wrong? Is it your illness?"

I went stiff. "It's not that, just having a weird day, but it's not that. And we can just say *kidney thing* since no one wants to pronounce the whole word."

She blushed and set her bag on the couch. "I'm sorry. I would hate someone looking at me and thinking of me being sick. I'll do my best not to do it to you."

I shook my head. "I got so used to everyone around me knowing that I was sick that I don't bring it up often."

"I guess. I still feel bad for bringing it up. But I will be watching you like a hawk." She paused a bit and put on a bright smile as she sat down. "I'm sure Mackenzie will, too."

And there it was. The little moments I had been missing all this time.

Jesus Christ, I was an idiot. And I didn't know how to fix it.

I sat down and set up my books. "You're right. She does take care of me. I try to take care of her, too, though."

"So, I guess it's getting serious between you," she said softly.

I froze, uneasy now.

"Well, I'm glad you two have each other. It's sort of surprising, though. It feels like it came out of the blue. I mean, she was just with Sanders, and then I blinked, and you guys were together."

I set my last book down. "And that's a good thing... I mean she and I, we're going very slowly."

"Of course, I'm happy for you."

She wasn't lying. I thought I could tell when she was lying. But there *was* something else, and I had missed it all this time.

She looked at me, and her face went pale.

"How did you find out?" Her voice cracked yet had a hollow ting to it that broke me.

"Nessa..." I began. She stood up quickly, her books falling to the floor. She held out her hand and promptly shoved everything back into her bag.

"It's fine. I'm fine. It's a stupid little thing that I'm going to get over. Seriously. I'm happy for you two, and I'm not being a sarcastic bitch about it. I promise. We're friends, Pacey. It's just been a bizarre couple of months. I need to get out of my head. But I will. I've got to go."

"Nessa."

She held up a hand. "Please, I just need a few minutes. We're not even really in any classes this semester, so maybe I should start studying with my other study groups."

My heart twisted. "We're friends, Nessa. That's not going to change."

"Of course, not. We hang out at parties and with groups. We're friends, Pacey. But now that Corinne's gone, and you and Mackenzie are..." Her voice broke. "I'm fine," she said again. "I just need a minute. Okay?" I reached out for her, but she brushed it away. "I need some time, Pace."

So I watched her walk away, closed the door behind her, and lowered my head, pinching the bridge of my nose.

So much had happened already this semester that I could barely keep up. It seemed all I did was make mistake after mistake. And it wasn't that I was keeping secrets. I was just so used to being my own person and not confiding in others that I ended up hurting people over and over again. I needed to do better.

"I told you I would hurt you if you hurt her," Miles said, surprising me. Miles was the quietest of all of us. Even though Tanner usually kept to himself and brooded more, Miles only spoke when he got nervous or, as I was coming to find out, when he was angry.

"I'm sorry," I said. He shook his head. "Don't apologize to me. What the fuck do you think you were doing, leading Nessa on like that?"

My eyes widened. "I didn't lead her on. I thought we were friends. Her, me, and Corinne. *Friends*. I didn't know that'd changed for her. I didn't see it. And maybe I'm an asshole for that, but I didn't make her any promises. Didn't *do* anything."

Miles narrowed his eyes but gave me a tight nod. "I know, I'd hit you right now if you had made a promise to her."

"And I'd probably watch him do it, just to see if he could," Tanner said, and Miles glared at him.

"Thanks for the vote of confidence."

"I try," Tanner drawled. "Nessa will be fine. She just needs to get over whatever ideals she has about you. But, Pacey? You keeping your illness from her and us and then suddenly dating Mackenzie like this? It's a lot."

I threw my hands into the air. "I wasn't keeping my illness from anyone. I was just sick. I don't tell everybody in the world I meet that, 'Hey, I had a kidney transplant.' Do you know what that's like? To have people stare at you, wondering if you're going to pass out at any moment?"

"You *did* pass out," Tanner said softly.

I closed my eyes and groaned. "I know. And I should have told you guys. Mostly so you could check on me to make sure I was okay. I'm glad you guys know now and that you know the signs to look for if I have a cold or something. But I'm okay. I swear. I just don't need to reveal my exact medical history to everybody all the time. It wasn't that I was keeping it a secret, it's just...my business," I said, getting angry.

"Fine," Miles said. "We'll deal. But Nessa's hurt, and while it might not have been your fault, you were blind because you're falling for Mackenzie. And that's something you need to deal with."

"I'm trying," I growled. "I'm fucking trying. But I'm not doing a very good job of it."

"No, you're not," Tanner said, shrugging.

"Why are you both so talkative all of a sudden?"

"Because we like you, you're our friend, and you keep fucking up."

I let out a breath. "Between school and the hospitalization, it's all too much. College isn't supposed to be this hard."

"You want a drink?" Tanner asked as he went to the bar.

"No..." I began. "I can't drink when I'm on my meds."

"Fine, I'll have two for you." He poured two drinks and gave one to Miles, who just smirked.

"Oh, so I wasn't going to get a drink if Pacey wanted one."

"No, I was going to pour them both for myself, but I figured since you were standing there, I should probably be nice."

"Thanks," Miles said and sighed. "I like Nessa."

My brows shot up. "Like?"

"As a friend, damn it. She's a good person. She just happens to like you, though I don't know why," Miles said with laughter in his eyes.

I flipped him off.

"It's the accent," Tanner said. "Chicks always go for the accent. I don't see it myself."

"You'd be lucky to get with me," I said, laughing.

"You wish. Sorry, I have enough drama in my life."

"You and the duo no longer a trio?" I asked, honestly interested.

Tanner leaned back against the wall and rolled his eyes. "Apparently. I think they wanted to go for a rhombus or some shit. And I'm all for being happy and doing what you want. However, I am more for honesty, so it's just my hands and me tonight."

"That's an image I'm never going to get out of my head."

I laughed. "I don't know what I'm supposed to do. All I keep doing is making mistakes."

"How can you fix them?" Miles asked.

"I don't know. I just...I can't tell everybody in the world that I'm sick. It's not their business, and hell, I don't want to be that guy."

"They don't need to know about that. Mackenzie did because she was there to help you, and I'm glad that we know now, but honestly, I'm not upset that you didn't tell us before," Tanner said, surprising me. "Seriously. It's none of our business. We can joke that you're mysterious and keep secrets with that accent of yours, but that's all it is: a joke. Now, you not seeing that Nessa liked you? I also get that. A lot of times, we don't see what's right in front of us."

I swallowed hard. "I never wanted to hurt Nessa. Ever. I also hate that Mackenzie is the one who figured it out because of the tension at the house."

Miles winced. "That can't be easy. Especially since I bet your girl already feels weird living with them."

"You know, that's very perceptive," I said, and Tanner snorted. "Miles is all nice and sweet and observant. I still don't know why he's single."

Miles flipped us both off. "I'm single because I have no time for women."

"Sure," Tanner said, though I knew he was just fucking with us both. We were exhausted, and frankly, I hadn't had enough time to just hang out with my roommates. Dillon was rarely here unless he was with Elise, and I hated that I barely got to see the one guy I had gotten closest to last semester. But I liked Tanner and Miles, and it was nice getting to know them a bit more, though I still didn't know all their secrets—they weren't mine to know. After all, I had just finished saying that I needed to keep things to myself.

Except there was one more thing I needed to talk about.

"Shit," I muttered and looked longingly at the drink in Tanner's hand.

"I'm not giving you this drink. Now, tell me what's wrong."

"There's one more thing you should probably know," I said and drained the now ice-cold tea that had been sitting in front of me.

"What?" Miles asked. "Is it your kidney? Because Dillon and I already talked, and we figured if we all got our blood typed, we could see if we could be here for you if you do need another kidney."

I looked at him then and choked. "Seriously?"

"Why didn't you ask me?" Tanner asked as he took another drink. "I'm only destroying my liver, not my kidneys."

That made me laugh, and thankfully, Miles joined in.

"Dillon and I just talked about it. All of us were actually going to do it, including Dillon's family if you were interested. I mean, we felt weird and didn't know what to do, so we thought we'd be annoying and in your face."

I swallowed hard, tears threatening. "That's kind of... that's bloody brilliant. I don't know if that's even an option, but I know that you could always be part of things like a bone marrow registry if you want to be proactive. I shouldn't need that, but my cousin did, and a random anonymous donor saved her life."

"Good to know," Tanner said. "Maybe. You know we're young, some of us are healthy, and we might as well help out, especially when we're all stressed. Now, tell us what the fuck's going on with you."

I went still, trying to form my thoughts. "There's one more secret you should probably know." I looked down at my hands and sighed.

"If you say you're cheating on Mackenzie, I may actually have to hurt you," Miles growled.

My eyes widened. "No, not that. Fuck. Okay. You know how we get the house for a bargain?" I began, wincing.

Tanner set his drink down. "If you fucking own this house, like the billionaire Mr. Body from *Clue*, I will have to murder you in the living room with the closest candlestick."

That made Miles burst out laughing, and I just shook my head before blurting. "I don't own it, but my aunt does."

"Are you fucking kidding me?" Miles asked, his eyes wide. "This is your family's home?"

"It's my aunt's home. And my mum, her sister, doesn't usually live in America, so it's not like it's a family home. However, she is giving us a good deal. Hence why we don't need to fill Sanders' room unless we want to. I'm sorry, I didn't know how to bring it up. I didn't want it to be an issue with you guys to begin with. And, yes, I will tell Dillon," I added quickly.

"Jesus Christ, how many more secrets do you have?" Tanner asked as he sat up.

"None. I swear. At least, I don't think so. Shit, I'm sorry."

"You're like one of the rich kids that used to make fun of me in school," Miles whispered.

I shook my head. "Just because my family has money doesn't mean I do."

"Got a trust fund?" Tanner asked as he down the rest of his drink.

I winced. "Hell, I'm sorry. I didn't want things to be weird between us, and all I did was make things weirder. I'm usually much better than this."

Tanner just glared at me. "Yeah, I guess you are. But, Mr. Moneybags, good to know where you come from, though we don't know how many more secrets you have."

I didn't understand Tanner's reaction, but as he stormed away, I stared at Miles. "I didn't know what to do. I didn't want you all thinking you needed to be beholden to me or something, and then it got weird."

Miles shook his head. "I don't know, maybe if you hadn't kept other things a secret, it wouldn't be such a big deal. Or maybe if it weren't happening with the whole Nessa thing, it wouldn't either. I don't know. But you know Tanner's got issues with money. And I've got issues with rich kids who pick on me—not that you're one of them."

"I'm not," I growled. "Just because someone has money doesn't make them a bully."

"Well, Sanders was, so I guess that doesn't help matters," Miles said as he stuck his hand in his pocket. "I don't blame you for not telling us. It would have been weird when we first met. But you've had a semester and a half now, Pacey."

"When was I supposed to bring it up? When Dillon was falling for Elise, and we were all stressed out about school? Or when we lost Corinne? Or maybe when I was passed out in an ambulance? I don't fucking know, everything just piled up, and I couldn't focus. I can't even talk to my parents about things because they're not talking to each other, and it's just fucking weird. And that's not even the point. I'm sorry."

Miles came up and squeezed my shoulder, surprising me.

"You're having a shit semester. I'm sorry, and I know not all of this is your fault. You can fix it. You always do."

"I've never had so much—and things like this—to fix before," I muttered.

"No, you haven't. So, figure it out. But, Pacey? You're going to have to fix things with Nessa and Tanner. You're probably going to have to tell Mackenzie about the house, too."

I groaned and sank back into the couch. "When did school get so hard?"

"This has nothing to do with school, Pacey. This is about who you are and the choices you want to make. So, you better figure it out. Because if you don't? You might not have anyone left to hurt, even by accident." And on that lovely note, Miles walked away and left me alone.

Apparently, I was really good at fucking things up today —or every day.

And I knew I deserved every ounce of anger I had for myself—as well as everybody else's anger that was currently directed my way.

Eighteen

Mackenzie

I STEPPED INTO MY DRESS AND PULLED IT UP OVER my chest so I could wrap the straps around my shoulders. The skirt flared out at the knees over my tights, and I figured it would have to do. It was getting slightly warmer out, but we were at that stage in the Colorado winters when it could feel like it was spring turning into summer one minute and then go straight back to winter the next, so I never counted my chickens early by dressing for full summer.

"You look cute," Natalie said as she came in and handed over a small wrap. "I borrowed this from you last week for one of the parties. I figured I should give it back. It will work with your outfit tonight."

I smiled and took it from her. "I was just thinking about this. Thank you."

"No problem. Thank you for letting me borrow it."

"I still can't believe I'm taking time to go on a date," I said, shaking my head.

"You and Pacey have been together nearly all semester at this point. You *should* be going out on dates."

I blinked, doing the math. "Wow, it *has* been over two months, hasn't it?"

"Yep. You guys are the talk of the town," she said, the look in her eyes teasing.

I shuddered. "Don't say that. I don't want to be the talk of any town."

"You're not," she said. "I promise. I was only teasing you."

"Good, after the whole scene with Sanders, well, the second scene that is, I'm not in the mood to be anybody's gossip call."

"I don't blame you. But you don't have to worry. Everyone's dealing with their own issues. And it's not like we're a super small campus or anything."

"Thank God for that." We met each other's gazes, and both smiled. "Anyway, you think this is fine for tonight?" I asked as I twirled a bit. "I'm not in the mood to show off too much of my legs, so I figured cute tights would work."

"I think you look gorgeous. And I'm sure Pacey will agree."

I grinned.

"You're so nice to me," I said. "Is Nessa still out?" I asked, my stomach tightening.

Natalie gave me a sad smile. "She is. She said that it's a study group, but I have a feeling it has more to do with a certain date you're going on tonight."

I held back a curse. "I was afraid you were going to say that. We need to sit down and talk because I don't want her to hate me."

Nessa's eyes widened. "She doesn't hate you. Believe me. I think she's just embarrassed."

I frowned. "Why would she feel that way?" I asked, honestly perplexed.

"Because she has a crush on a guy who's dating her roommate and friend."

"She shouldn't be embarrassed. We all have crushes that sometimes go unrequited."

Natalie blushed, and I wondered what that was about. "Well, I think she just needs some space."

"I'm trying to give her that, but we are roommates. We share a house."

"And she's trying not to show her pain to anyone," Natalie said kindly.

"I should have realized that something was going on before I asked Pacey to be my rebound."

"He's not your rebound anymore, is he?" she asked, and I shook my head. "No, I don't think he is. I don't know what he is, but I don't think he's that."

"It is exciting in a way, you and Pacey."

I shrugged, looking down at my hands. "Maybe. I don't know. I went from one serious relationship to something I thought would only be fun. And maybe it should continue being that way. But I don't know. We're not good about talking about what we're feeling."

"You know, I don't think most people are," Natalie said honestly. I looked up at her. "Seriously. In movies and books, we tell people, 'You just need to talk and tell them how you feel.' But in real life? Do we do that? No. We hide, and we get embarrassed, and if someone announces how they feel, we think they're either coming on too strong or will feel horrible later. Sometimes, you need to take your time and think about it, not just blurt out what you're thinking."

I smiled.

"You're right. And I need to remember to live in the moment. We only have a little over a year of school left. I can't live my entire life surrounded by boys."

"You're not," she said.

I rolled my eyes. "It sure feels like it. I spent the first two and a half years of college with Sanders, and now here I am, two months in with Pacey. Boys, boys, boys."

"While going to school, dealing with thesis issues, kicking ass in those classes, finding a new home, making friends, and doing a thousand little things for others. You're rocking it, and it's not just about boys."

"Thank you for that."

"You're welcome. I mean, sometimes I would like my life to be about boys, but I will forever be the virgin of the group," she said and smiled softly.

"Have you wanted to date?" I asked honestly.

"Not really. I haven't found anyone that I want to take on and deal with." She rolled her eyes. "And that sounds horrible. But I don't know, I've just been busy, and finding someone to even enjoy some time with seems like a big thing right now. I'd rather focus on school and see what happens."

"That's smart. I mean, look what happens when you start dating someone, and things get super complicated."

"Things might be complicated, but you're happy. Remember that."

At that moment, Nessa came up behind Natalie, her eyes wide. I almost cursed, but instead, I looked up and smiled.

"Hi, Nessa," I said.

"You look great," Nessa said and held up something shiny. "When I saw you, I thought of these." My eyes widened as she handed over some dangly earrings. "What do you think? Will they work?"

I looked at them and then at her. My heart swelled, even as it twisted a bit. We were all trying so hard to be okay with everything, but feelings were feelings, and you couldn't make them go away. Were these earrings an olive branch? If so, I'd take them.

"They're beautiful." I took out the studs I had on and slid on the shiny little dangly pieces, smiling into the mirror.

"Corinne bought them for me," Nessa said softly, and Natalie discreetly wiped a tear as I looked over at Nessa.

I swallowed hard, my throat tight. "Nessa, thank you."

She just shrugged, her smile a bit sad. "She had great taste. And so do you. I just wanted to say have fun tonight. Seriously."

I wanted to reach out, do something. Instead, I simply blinked away tears and smiled. "Thank you."

"You're welcome. Now, don't be late because we both know how Pacey hates tardiness," she said and then winced. "Is this weird?" she asked.

I shook my head. "Not if we don't want it to be or make it weird. Not that we would ever want it to be. And that's a strange thing to say," I said and put my hands over my face. "I suck at this."

"Oh, I think I'm worse. Now, I am going to study because I have an exam coming up and I haven't been focusing as I should. But, seriously, have fun." She gave a little wave and went off to her room.

Natalie stood in the corner, frozen like a statue, her eyes wide. And then she held up two thumbs and grinned.

I smiled back and figured that I was one step closer to the friendship I wanted. At least, I hoped so.

Dinner with Pacey was excellent.

We shared a small pizza from an actual wood oven, as well as a side of pasta with cheese. I was so full, I felt like I could burst. Now, we walked towards his house, his arm wrapped around me as I leaned into his side.

"Thank you for driving," Pacey said, and I laughed.

"It was my turn to drive. So sorry you had to deal with me picking you up and dropping you off."

"I'm just sad you didn't bring flowers, so Tanner could continue giving me that shit-eating grin."

"I thought about it, but they're not in my budget right now."

Pacey smiled. "It's fine. I'll send some to myself on your behalf to make Tanner smile."

That made me laugh. "Anything to make Tanner smile."

Pacey walked me inside, and I waved at Miles where he sat playing video games on the couch.

"Have fun tonight, you two?" he asked, and I leaned into Pacey, carb-happy.

"Yes," I said after a moment.

"What she isn't saying is that we are in carb heaven right now. And I think I gained twenty pounds."

I laughed at Pacey. "Well, I wasn't going to tell Miles that. But we did bring leftovers," I said and handed him a pizza box. "We ate all the pasta."

Miles' eyes widened. "For me?"

"We also have some for Tanner and Dillon," Pacey said softly, holding up another bag.

"I would have brought some for the girls, but well, I wasn't sure when I'd be getting back to my place," I said quickly and ducked my head. I hadn't meant to say that out loud. When Miles' gaze brightened, I ignored it.

Why didn't I just tell him that I wasn't going home in the morning because I would be having sex with Pacey tonight? I probably should have just said that.

Miles winked and took the pizza. "Oh, it's still hot. Hell, yeah. Now I know what I'm having for my after-dinner snack."

"Half a pizza?" I asked, laughing.

"Don't judge," he said before taking out an enormous slice. Miles was bigger than the rest of the guys, wider with more muscle, though I didn't know when he had time to work out. He was the one I could never quite put my finger on. Sometimes, he was geeky. Other times, he was growly. And a lot of times, he acted like the skinny kid in the corner with no friends. Yet he was the exact opposite of that most days.

I liked him and was glad that he was my friend. Especially since he had sort of been friends with Sanders when they were roommates, and I was afraid that he might have taken Sanders' side. I shouldn't have thought that, and I felt bad about it now. But everything was fine. We dropped off the rest of the pizza in the fridge with notes for the guys and made our way upstairs. I leaned into Pacey, happy and sated and trying not to feel weird that everyone would know what we were doing. However, everyone had known before with Sanders. It was just what happened when you had room-mates in college. People knew way too much about your sex life.

"Where are those thoughts of yours going?" Pacey asked softly. I looked up at him and gave a small smile. "Just thinking about everyone knowing exactly what we're doing in here."

He grinned. "Oh, and what exactly *are* we doing today?"

"Nothing," I said and bit my lip.

"Well, let me think. Could it be this?" he asked as he pressed a kiss to my neck. I shivered.

"Maybe."

"What about this?" he asked, and I swallowed hard as he kissed the other side of my neck.

"What about this?" he added before pressing a kiss to the swell of my breast.

My knees shook, and I gripped his arms. "Pacey," I whispered. My head fell back as he gently placed another kiss on my other breast. "Pacey..."

"I need you," he growled.

"Then take me."

He slowly began stripping me of my clothes, carefully taking off my wrap and my dress. The fabric pooled on the floor, leaving me in my bra and tights as I pressed myself against his length.

He groaned and looked down at me before he dropped to his knees in front of me. He kissed my center over my tights before slowly pulling them down, taking his time as he played with my ass. I wiggled in his hold, needing him.

"You're so damn beautiful," he groaned before kissing my clit.

My knees went weak, and I gripped his shoulders for balance. He lapped at me, and I moaned, needing support. Then he pushed me back onto the couch, my legs in the air as I let out a breath. He licked and sucked until I fought to catch my breath. When he looked up at me, his blond hair disheveled, his mouth wet from my pussy, I came. I couldn't help it. He grinned before going back to tasting me, and I did my best not to fall off the couch. I was on the precipice, near the edge of something I couldn't quite name. I'd already come, but I was almost there again, needing release. Needing something. Needing Pacey.

I knew I already loved this man, and yet I couldn't tell him.

I could barely admit it to myself.

And when he finally pulled away to strip and put on a condom, I looked up at him, licking my lips.

"Take off the bra and bend over the couch. I'm going to fuck you so hard you'll scream my name loudly enough for the neighbors to hear."

I should have blushed. I should have said no.

Instead, I did as he directed. I couldn't help it. I needed more.

I needed him.

My bra dropped to the side as I settled myself on my knees on the couch, holding on for dear life as Pacey thrust into me with one eager movement, his cock stretching me to the point of pain yet bringing me closer to bliss.

"My God. You're so fucking tight, Mackenzie. I'm going to come right here."

"I need...move. Fuck me."

I was never this brazen. Never this willing to voice my needs. Yet, I could be different with Pacey. I could be the woman I thought of in my head, rather than the one afraid of what others might say.

I looked over my shoulder as he rode me, my breasts swaying, my body shaking. He had his hands on my hips, his fingers digging in hard enough to leave bruises. He leaned over me, his body hard and sweat-slick as he captured my mouth with his. My pussy clenched, my entire core vibrating to the point of near pain. And with that one kiss, I fell.

I didn't just come. I screamed, shook. I fell harder than I ever thought possible.

He came with me, urging us both past the point of bliss and into an eternity of something I couldn't quite grasp.

This wasn't what I had planned. This wasn't where I thought I'd be.

And yet, I loved him.

I loved Pacey Ziglar.

And I was so damn scared that I was making another mistake.

Even as he held me, took care of me.

I was afraid.

Again.

Nineteen

Pacey

I set out deli meat and crusty French bread on the kitchen island before going back to the fridge to find mustard and mayonnaise.

"What's this?" Miles asked as he walked in. I looked over my shoulder to see my roommate licking his lips.

"We are all studying for finals, and that means we need sustenance. I figured I'd splurge on decent thin pastrami and rare roast beef, as well as some honey-cured ham and brown sugar turkey."

"Dear God, marry me," Miles said, and I laughed.

"Well, that's a proposal I wasn't expecting," Dillon said as he grinned.

"Hell, yeah, this looks awesome. Is this why you wanted

me to pick up four types of pickles and pepperoncinis?" he asked as he set the bag next to me.

"Did you go right down the list?"

Dillon just rolled his eyes. "What do you take me for? Of course, I went through the list. Though I have to say, it reminded me of Mackenzie. It's a little weird how much you start acting like your significant other over time. How long has it been now? Four, five months?"

I rolled my eyes. "You and Elise are the same. And I think it's been four, maybe four and a half? Shit, I'm usually better at remembering things like that, but I've been a little busy." I'd had another attack the month prior, thanks to a sinus infection gone wrong, but I hadn't been hospitalized. I just had to miss a week of classes again. Mackenzie had helped me, though, as had the rest of my roommates. The fact that her soap was in my shower had not escaped me. I had a serious girlfriend, who I loved, but still hadn't told that because I didn't think we were there yet. After all, I was only supposed to be her rebound. I didn't need to strip myself bare, only to have her say it was fun for the semester, but now she was moving on. Everyone told me that she needed time to find her way as a single woman and a person, and yet, she had somehow ended up with me right away.

That meant she and I couldn't be serious.

And I was lying to myself.

"Everything okay?" Miles asked, and I nodded.

"Yes, exams are going to suck. And so are papers, so let's eat."

"Do you have chips?" Tanner asked, and I narrowed my eyes at him.

"Of course, I have crisps. What do you take me for?"

"I don't know, I worry about these things," Tanner said with a grin.

"Yes, they're kettle crisps, the kind with jalapeño for you."

"Hell, yeah," Tanner said as he made his way to the pantry.

"Seriously, I'm probably going to eat all of this myself, so I don't know what you guys are going to do," Miles added as he started building himself a sandwich. I laughed and did the same. Soon, all of us were pretty much cleaning out my double sandwich inventory and chowing down while standing around the island. Dillon had given me the stool, and Tanner was leaning on one. If we continued living here for another year, and with the girls in and out as much as they were, we probably needed another set of stools for the kitchen area.

"Now, what are you thinking?" Miles asked as he bit into a pepperoncini. He went to reach for another one. They were the extra-hot ones, and I was surprised he didn't beg for some milk.

"I just thought we needed more stools in here since the girls are over so often."

"Yeah, Mackenzie and Elise do spend a lot of time here," Tanner said, his brows raised.

"Well, they don't spend the night every night. They still live with Natalie and Nessa."

None of us mentioned that Nessa wasn't spending as much time here as she had in the past. We still saw each other, but she refused to study with me, and I hated myself just a bit for that. I had screwed everything up because I hadn't seen what was going on, and things were slightly awkward now. I had tried to apologize, but she wouldn't listen. She had said she needed space, so I was giving that to her. Even if I still felt like a piece of shit for hurting her in the first place.

"What's your first exam?" Miles asked, and I blinked, realizing he was talking to me.

"Um, statistical analysis and everything else that's in that title that I can never remember." I laughed as the guys crossed their eyes at me.

"In other words, Dr. Michael's class. He's the asshole professor, not the evil one," I said, and Dillon shook his head. "You know, I always thought I was decent at math, then I met you and Mackenzie. I'm happy that I do not have to take those courses."

"These are my last main math courses," I said. It's only my minor. Next year's all physics, all the time."

"Are you going to be able to take fewer credit hours, then?"

I shook my head, "Nope. Labs are only one credit hour. That means I get to spend even more hours on campus and yet not get as many credits for it. I love our system."

"Sometimes, I feel like I should've just gone to culinary school as planned," Dillon said to me, and I nodded. "Between you and Tanner, you eat well. I usually provide sandwiches," I said with a laugh, and Miles shrugged. "They're damn good sandwiches," he said, taking his final bite of a pastrami on rye.

"I don't want to get back to studying," Tanner said, "It's hard to believe that we're nearly done with our third year."

"Fourth year's coming up fast," I said, shaking my head.

"Well, I guess we should go study so we can pass our

classes and not end up with extra semesters," Dillon said. "As it is, I was afraid I might not graduate on time since I took a year off and fucked around. But I'm here, and who needs sleep?"

"Well, considering you spend most of your time in bed with Elise, I guess you don't," Tanner said and ducked Dillon's playful punch.

We started cleaning up the dishes, all of us talking about our random classes until Dillon cleared his throat.

"Hey, I just want you to know that even though we haven't talked about it with you, we're okay that your aunt owns this place," he said, and I looked to see Tanner and Miles nodding.

It seemed they'd made Dillon their spokesperson. I didn't mind that too badly.

"I am sorry I didn't tell you. I didn't know how to bring it up."

"Of course, you didn't," Dillon said.

"Anyway, I don't know if I can convince my aunt to lower the rent, but I think we do okay."

"Our rent is ridiculously low already," Tanner said. "We don't need charity." At the tone of his voice, I nodded and dropped the subject.

"Okay, Tanner, I have to go write this paper. It'll be the end of me," Miles said as he dried his hands. "You think I'm dramatic enough?"

"Yes." I shook my head. We made our way back to our respective study areas just as the doorbell rang. I frowned.

"Are we expecting anyone?" I asked.

"The girls are all sitting at their place but are coming

over for dinner. At least, Elise and Mackenzie are," Dillon added quickly.

Nessa was still being cautious, which meant Natalie wasn't coming over as much either so Nessa didn't feel left out. It was an awkward situation. One I intended to fix. And from the way Miles glared at me, I knew I would have to fix it soon.

I went to open the door and gritted my teeth.

"Father," I said. My dad gave me a small smile.

"I thought we could talk." I looked over at my father's girlfriend and gave her a tight nod.

"Finals week is coming up. I really don't have time," I said softly.

"Please, son," my dad said. I swallowed hard and let him in.

"We can go back to the kitchen. My roommates are studying."

"We can head to our rooms," Dillon called, and I gave him a small shake of the head.

"No, it's fine. You guys don't need to leave."

"Are you going to introduce me to your roommates, son?" my father asked, his voice as proper as ever.

"Why? I don't know if you're going to be staying that long, Dad."

"I'm Jessica," my father's girlfriend said and waved at the guys.

They just blinked, and Miles waved awkwardly before lowering his hand.

"Fine. Miles, Dillon, Tanner, this is my father and his pregnant girlfriend. My parents are still married, though I think they just separated. And as they're both in the United

States at the moment, they're not even separated by an ocean. Yes, this is my father's girlfriend. And I'm pretty sure she's near my age."

"Pacey," my dad snapped.

My head shot up. "What? You haven't called or texted or done anything since that dinner and when I got sick. What do you expect me to say right now?"

"Your mom gave me updates on your health. I was updated."

I pinched the bridge of my nose. "You made my mother deal with you after you cheated on her? So you could get updates about me rather than just talking to me yourself?"

"I didn't think you'd receive me well. Clearly, I was right."

I could hear the guys leaving, and Jessica shifted from foot to foot, her hands on her ever-growing stomach. I didn't know how far along she was, but she wasn't in her first trimester anymore for sure.

I didn't even know what they planned to name the kid.

"I just want you to tell me why," I said.

"Why? Jessica and I get each other," my dad answered as he wrapped his arms around her waist. She looked up at him dreamily, and I wanted to throw up. "Your mother and I went through some hard times. She didn't understand what I needed. But I love you, Pacey. And this baby in here will be your little sister. She's going to need you."

I swallowed hard. "A sister. And you couldn't even put that in a text. I'm going to have a fucking sister, and I don't even know this woman." I cringed and looked at Jessica. "I'm sure you're a nice lady, but you did help my dad cheat on my mum, so I'm not going to have good feelings about you right now."

She blanched, and I cursed.

"Pacey!"

"You know what? You should probably go. I can't deal with this right now. I have things to do, and it's already been a tough enough semester. I don't need to deal with you, too."

"Pacey, some things are just better kept private."

I threw my hands into the air. "You say that, and yet the more things I keep to myself, the harder it is when people find out about them. You should be open and honest. Why the hell did you cheat on mum?"

"Because I didn't love her anymore."

I took a step back and swallowed hard. "I thought you did. You guys waxed poetic about each other for my entire life. You're the reason I thought relationships could be functional and extend into adulthood, rather than everyone getting divorced as all my friends' parents did."

"Pacey, maybe one day when you fall in love, you'll realize that it can fade."

I growled, actually growled. "You need to go. I'll talk to you soon, but I can't focus on you right now. There's too much else going on, and you're just making the stress worse." I looked at Jessica. "Really, I'm sure you're a lovely person. And once I figure out what the hell I'm thinking, I want to get to know my baby sister. But you need to go now. My dad broke up his marriage, but he wasn't alone. You need to go."

"Mark my words, Pacey, you'll understand what it means when I say that love doesn't always mean forever." The fact that my father could say that while holding his girlfriend made me want to shout, but I didn't. Instead, I just stood there, my chest heaving and my lungs burning. Shit, the more stress I took on, the harder it was for me to stay healthy.

And this certainly wasn't helping.

My dad gave me one last look before turning on his heel and barreling out, nearly knocking Mackenzie over.

She looked at me, her face pale. I had a feeling she had heard most of that.

"Pacey," she whispered.

"Please, go," I said, closing my eyes. My throat hurt. Everything hurt. I just wanted it all to end for a moment. "I need you to go for now. I can't handle this. Or you. Or anyone."

I looked up, and she just blinked at me, her lips parted. "You don't want me to stay..." she whispered.

"Just go, okay? Just go."

TWENTY

Mackenzie

"JUST GO."

I blinked at Pacey, trying to figure out what the hell had just happened.

"Pacey," I said, my voice coming out shakier than I wanted.

"I can't do this right now," he said and rubbed his chest.

My eyes widened, and I moved forward. "Are you okay? What's wrong? Do you need to sit down?"

He shook his head and held out his hand to block me. "I can't do this right now, Mackenzie. It's all too much. I need a minute. I need you to leave."

I looked at him then, trying to understand why he was pushing me away.

"What just happened? Let me help."

"It's too much. You didn't ask for this. Whatever is going on right now isn't what we signed up for. You need to go."

Cold surged through my body, and a trickle of memory and unease took root as I tried to form the thoughts I needed to become the woman I had to be in that instant. Why did it feel like I was breaking? *I shouldn't be.* He wasn't breaking up with me. What the hell was going on? And why did it feel like a chasm was opening inside me, trying to steal my last breath?

"You keep repeating those words. Yet you won't tell me *why*. Why are you acting like this?" I shook my head, my soul twisting as if it were a shield trying to protect me. "I'm not going to leave, Pace. We don't do that. We *stay*."

He rubbed his hands down his face, his breathing labored. "That was my father right there. And his pregnant girlfriend. Trying to...I don't even know. He hasn't contacted me this entire time. Not since I found out about Jessica. Do you get that? He didn't even want to see me after I was in the hospital. My *dad*. The guy who was always there for me growing up, no matter what. I thought he loved my mum. That he could do anything. They're the reason I thought relationships could work, no matter what. But I was wrong. They can't. When I told Dillon that he and Elise could work through anything as long as they communicated, I was wrong about that, too. I had to be. Because if my parents can't work things out, how the hell is anyone else supposed to?"

I shook my head, trying to make sense of his words. He was clearly panicking, the stress of the moment etched on his features to the point I wasn't sure I could calm him down.

"Your parents didn't work out because of their relationship. It's not on anyone else, Pacey. It's not on you."

He ran his hand through his hair, his arms tensing as he started to pace. "Maybe. Or perhaps they just stuck together for me. I'll never know because Dad changed the rules. Changed everything. And now he's here, and I can't deal with it. I can't deal with anything right now. We have fucking exams, Mackenzie. We're supposed to figure out who to be in the world, and I can't even take a fucking breath right now."

Alarm shot through me, and I took a step forward. The last time he couldn't breathe, I'd watched him fight to live as he rode next to me in the ambulance. "Pacey...is it something else? Talk to me."

He shook his head. "I can't focus, Mackenzie. I can't be the person you need me to be. Hell, I shouldn't have been that person anyway."

I swallowed hard, my chin rising, my blood turning to ice. "You don't mean that."

"We were supposed to be together for what? A night? I was supposed to be your rebound. And look what I did, I clung, like I always do. And now you're here, dealing with my shit when you have enough to deal with on your own. How have I helped you? How have I done anything for you other than pull you down and stand in your way? I even took your access to an internship. I did all of that."

I stiffened, my breaths coming in pants as I tried not to panic. "No, you didn't. Why are you saying things like this? It doesn't make any sense."

Pacey ran his hands through his hair and continued to pace. I didn't know if the other guys were upstairs listening or if they were out, but I couldn't focus on them right now. I could only stare at Pacey and acknowledge that I didn't understand why he was pushing me away.

"I think we're past a rebound, Mackenzie. You need to go and figure out who you're going to be, just like you planned. You told me yourself that you figured you should be single someday. Even before you asked me to be your rebound, you said you needed to figure out who you are. Yet, here I am, standing in your way. You should leave before one of us gets hurt."

"That's not how this works, Pacey." I knew I was repeating myself, but I couldn't think of what else to say. If I left...would it be forever? Would this be the end? A break? A moment to breathe? I didn't know.

"Maybe it's how it should be. You should go, Mackenzie. Save yourself. Escape my drama. You have enough, and I couldn't help you. I can't even help myself." He looked at me, then shook his head. "All I do is hurt people. Nessa, my roommates. I keep secrets, I try to protect myself, and I think I'm protecting others, but all I do is hurt them."

"Then why are you trying to hurt me now?" I asked and swallowed hard, annoyed that my voice broke.

"I'm not. I'm trying to *help* you."

"You're doing a shitty job." I looked at him then, saw how still he was, so withdrawn. He wasn't going to listen to me. He wasn't going to do anything. He was hurting, and there was nothing I could do right now. But he was right; everything around us was twisted and broken. I couldn't help him. Not yet.

"I'm not going away forever," I whispered.

Relief and pain flashed in his eyes. I wanted to reach out,

but I knew he would push me away again. And, honestly, I didn't know if I was strong enough to handle that. Not after Sanders. And I knew I couldn't do it for Pacey at all. Not when he meant so much more than Sanders ever did.

But Pacey didn't say anything. Instead, he just stood there and stared at me, looking so lost. And there was nothing I could do. So, I turned and I made my way to my car.

Pacey didn't come for me.

He didn't follow.

I didn't know how I made it back to the house. My tears fell freely, and I wiped them away furiously, annoyed that I'd even let them fall. This wasn't the end. It couldn't be. Pacey was hurt, lashing out. Something he never did. And he wasn't letting me help.

But I would. I had to find a way.

I staggered inside, swallowed hard, and ran into Nessa. She looked at me, her eyes wide, and she put her hands on my shoulders. "What's wrong? What happened?"

"Pacey," I blurted, choking on my sobs.

"Is he okay? Oh my God, do we have to go back to the hospital?"

I shook my head, rolled my shoulders back, and told myself to get it together.

"No, he's fine. At least, I think so. Physically, at least. I'm sorry, I didn't mean to worry you."

Nessa moved forward, alarm and worry carved on her features. "What's wrong?"

I wiped my tears and pulled away. Nessa was the last

person I should talk to. Not because I didn't adore her or think she wasn't my friend but because I didn't want to hurt her.

"It's nothing. I'll deal with it. But thank you."

"Don't lie to me. What's wrong with you?" Nessa shook her head. "What's wrong? You can talk to me. I promise."

I swallowed hard. "Pacey's going through a lot, and I think he just broke up with me," I said, my voice oddly hollow.

Nessa sighed and held out her arms. "Come on, let me hold you."

"I don't want it to be weird for you. I've hated that this has been weird for you for a month now. Probably longer. I didn't know, Nessa. I swear. I didn't realize until it was too late, and I didn't want to bring it up because I didn't want to hurt you. I don't. And now I'm doing it anyway, and I'm so sorry."

Nessa gave me a small smile and squeezed my hand. "It's not your fault that you fell in love with Pacey Ziglar. You're not alone there," she said.

"Damn it, Nessa. I wasn't supposed to fall in love. But I did. I haven't even been able to tell him. And maybe I should have, but perhaps it's good that I didn't. Because now it won't hurt as much if this is over. Baring my soul and aching for someone who doesn't love me will only hurt worse in the end. It was only supposed to be a rebound. I wasn't supposed to fall in love again. I thought I had my entire future planned out, and now, everything's unraveling. School, my summer internship, possibly my future. Everything I thought I had with Sanders. It's all gone; somehow got tangled up in Pacey. I thought maybe I could make things work, but now I think I'm just one more thing that's too much for him."

I tried to stop the sobs as the words tumbled out, but Nessa continued holding me, rubbing her hand up and down my back to soothe us both.

"Pacey is good at keeping things to himself. He's good at making sure everyone else has what they need, even if they don't realize it's what's needed. But he doesn't share every part of himself. He doesn't talk about Corinne with me," she whispered. My eyes filled with tears, and she continued.

"I know you feel weird when we bring her up, but you also bring her up because I know you're on the same page with us in keeping her memory alive."

I hugged Nessa, knowing she was in just as much—perhaps even *more*—pain. "Of course. I liked Corinne, too. And, yes, sometimes I feel like the fourth wheel or as if I'm taking her spot, but I'm not." I added quickly.

Nessa gave me a small smile. "We all know that. And we're making new memories in this home. Together. And, Pacey? They were friends, just like he and I are friends. But I made the lousy decision to fall in love with him. Or maybe I fell in love with the guy I thought he was. Because if I truly loved him, shouldn't he have noticed?"

"Guys can be stupid," I added, and she gave me a wry smile.

"That is true. I need to talk with Pacey, eventually. Because I miss my friend. But I don't want you to ever think that I would stand in the way of you two. I've seen how he looks at you. The way you look at him. There's something there. A happiness that I could never have with him."

"Nessa…" I began, my heart threatening to shatter into a million pieces. She shook her head.

"I know what falling for Pacey feels like, and I'm sorry that I ever made you feel like I hated you or wanted to push you away or made you feel bad for loving him. My feelings are *my* responsibility. Pacey will get his head out of his ass, take a deep breath, and realize what he did. It's not over between you two—it can't be."

"I don't know what's between us. What it should have been, or what it turned into. This semester has been a lot, Nessa. And it's only been a few months. Maybe he's right? Maybe space will help."

I was crying now, and Nessa squeezed my hand. "Maybe it'll all work out. We have to believe that. Because Pacey is my best friend, even if things are weird right now. And he loves you, I know it."

I wanted to believe her. Wanted to believe everything she was saying. But it was all twisted up.

So much had happened this semester that I couldn't keep up. And I was falling…failing.

Nothing was going the way I planned. And as someone who needed those pathways to function, I felt like I was numb. That nothing I did was right.

Pacey was hurt, and in his anxiousness, he pushed me away.

I wasn't sure what I was supposed to do about that. Or if I was supposed to do anything at all.

TWENTY-ONE

Pacey

I WAS SUCH A BLOODY IDIOT. SO MUCH SO THAT I knew that if I weren't careful, if I didn't plead and beg, I would lose everything.

I needed to be better. I needed to stop doing whatever the hell it was I was doing this year. So, I stood in front of Mackenzie's place and let out a breath. I didn't have anything with me. No flowers or chocolates or anything traditional would fix this.

At least, that's what I told myself. I needed to apologize. Let her know that I knew I was a fucking idiot. And maybe she would be better off without me. I had been right when I said that she had so much going on that my issues would only pile on for her. But I didn't need to be an asshole about it.

I hadn't needed to hurt her.

I'd kicked Mackenzie out. Rattled on about my problems and hadn't leaned on her. She didn't need me to do that. She needed more than a guy who put all of his issues on her. But I hadn't needed to be an asshole. Still, I had been.

And damn it, I hated myself for it.

I knocked on the door, unsure of my welcome. The door opened, and I blinked, not seeing the person I expected. Yet, it was someone else I needed to apologize to. Nessa gave me a small smile and shook her head. "She's not here. She had a meeting at school."

I swallowed hard. "Oh," I said. "That's good. I mean, well…" I added and shook my head. "Shit, I used to be good at this," I mumbled. She gave me a small smile.

"You used to be. But I know you're not right now. Why don't you come in? I think we need to talk anyway." She took a deep breath and straightened her shoulders. I nodded, my hands at my sides. I didn't know what to say, but I did know that I needed to apologize to Nessa for being a blind jerk. I had made so many mistakes this semester—for probably longer than that—and I needed to figure out how to fix them.

"I've wanted to talk to you for a while now," I began as I looked at her. "I've wanted to tell you so much, but I knew you needed some space."

Nessa studied my face, her gaze penetrating yet soft at the same time. "I'm glad you gave me time to reflect. And you're right, I needed to think about what I felt and figure out what I needed to say. I'm glad you didn't talk to me right away. Even though I have missed you."

I gave her a slight nod. "I've missed you, too, Nessa. I

hate that this semester seems to have blown up, to the point where I don't even know who I am anymore."

And that was the truth. I didn't. I had been the man with firm convictions until what I thought was true, shattered. I'd thought my parents loved each other and were an example for me, but I had been so very wrong in that respect. Wholly inaccurate. And then I thought I had a handle on my health, on who I wanted to be, and the path I needed to take. But *everything* had changed this semester. I no longer had to do things alone or think I needed to be strong and hide certain aspects of myself. But I still wasn't making the best decisions when it came to the people I loved. That was on me, and I needed to figure out how to fix it.

Because I loved Nessa, just not how she needed me to. And I didn't know how to change that. I didn't know how to make things better.

But I was here, and I hoped that would be enough—or at least the beginning.

"Well," she said, "I just wanted to say I'm sorry."

My eyes watered. "What on Earth do you have to be sorry about?"

She rolled her eyes and glared at me. "It's not all on you, Pacey. I hope you realize that. You don't have to take on the world just because you think you're responsible for everything."

I frowned and shook my head. "That's not it at all."

"I bet you were just thinking a whole little rant about how you needed to be better and how this is all about you. You're mistaken. It's not. I can make my own decisions, Pacey. I'm responsible for my feelings."

I winced. "But I shouldn't have had my head so far up my ass that I missed it."

"Don't you think that maybe I didn't want you to know? I mean, hell, Pacey, I knew you didn't think about me the same way." She was blushing so hard now that I wanted to reach out and hug her, tell her that everything would be okay. But I knew it wasn't my right, and it would probably just make things even more awkward.

"Life would have been so much easier if I hadn't had random thoughts that I knew wouldn't amount to anything. Because you were my friend, Pacey. And I don't say that word lightly, even though we tend to throw it around these days. I loved spending time with you and Corinne. But she's gone. And I hate that more every day, just like Elise does because we can't fix it. Even though I strongly want to."

I swallowed hard and nodded, my chest constricting. "I know. It's not easy."

"Of course, you had to go and fall for the new girl. One that I like." She wiped away a tear, and I reached out. She shook her head. "I'm not bothered that you have feelings for Mackenzie, Pacey. That was never the issue. I like her. I do. I think you two are great for each other. I'm responsible for whatever feelings I still have, not you. That much I can promise you."

I stared at her, wondering what I was supposed to say to that because there was nothing good about this. Nothing could make it better.

"I should have seen."

"And what would have happened if you had?" Nessa asked. "Would you have loved me back, Pacey? Would you have fallen for me because you thought it was the right thing to do? Or would you have felt awkward and not know what to say? Because I didn't make it obvious, at least I hoped I didn't, and just because I was weird about certain things doesn't mean you had to do anything about it."

I studied her face, wanting to reach out and hold my friend again, tell her that everything would be okay, even when I wasn't sure it could be. "I don't want anything to change, Nessa."

She smiled sadly. "We both know things changed long ago—and probably for the better."

"So, where do we go from here?" I asked softly.

"Wherever we need to. But I don't want to lose you as my friend. Even if things might be uncomfortable for a while."

I moved forward and gripped her hand. "I promise I'll try not to be a jerk anymore."

She froze for a minute and then smiled at me. "You were never a jerk, Pacey. That wasn't the problem. However, you didn't come here for me," she whispered.

I straightened. "Maybe I should have," I said.

"No, I needed space. And you gave it to me. Only today, you came here for Mackenzie."

I pulled away, pushing my hair out of my face.

"You know I used to be better about this. About reading people and figuring out what others needed. Now, look at me, screwing up over and over again because I can't focus."

"Maybe you're just overwhelmed. And you're allowed to make mistakes, you know. Despite what my imaginary version of you says, you're not perfect, Pacey. None of us are."

"Thanks for that," I said wryly.

"You love her, don't you?" she asked, her voice soft.

I swallowed hard. "I think I do," I said. "I'm sorry if that hurts you."

She shook her head and held up a hand. "This isn't about me. If you love her, that's great. I need to get out of my head. I know that. But you're not getting rid of *me* that easily. We're going to be the eight musketeers or whatever we are now between our two households, no matter what happens. But that means you need to talk to Mackenzie. Just talk."

My lips twitched, even as frustration crawled over me. "Shit, I know. That's why I'm here."

"Then find her on campus because she's pretty amazing, Pace. And I want you to be together. Even if some part of me feels like an idiot."

"You were never an idiot, Nessa."

"Maybe not. But as I said, I'm responsible for my thoughts and feelings."

I stared at her then, not knowing what else to say. "We're okay?" I asked, feeling like an idiot.

She smiled. "Of course. We're friends because we're friends, nothing more, nothing less. And not because of my wrong and weird feelings. Now, I'm going to kick you out. Not because I'm angry or weird—even though I am weird, but that's beside the point."

That made me snort because she sounded like the old Nessa, the one I had hurt with my incompetence.

"Go, find her. You two are meant for each other."

I sighed and pulled her close for a hug. She stiffened for a moment, and I was afraid that I had made the wrong move, but then she wrapped her arms around me and hugged me back.

"You're my friend, Nessa."

"Yeah, I am," she said with a smile I felt against my shoulder and then let go, leading me towards the door. And Mackenzie.

And, hopefully, my future.

TWENTY-TWO

Mackenzie

I WAS ONCE AGAIN RUNNING LATE, AND WHILE I didn't want to be *that* student flailing as she ran across campus, I figured I might need to be soon if I didn't pick up the pace.

Dr. Michaels had emailed me that morning, telling me that I needed to meet with him for something vital. Just because he wasn't my favorite person didn't mean I would blow him off. So that meant I had to shower and try to look presentable since I had been wallowing in my pajamas and covered in junk food for nearly a full day, as I studied and pretended like Pacey hadn't pushed me out of his house like I was nothing. Okay, that wasn't exactly what he had done, but that's what it'd felt like in the moment. And I wasn't feeling particularly charitable to anyone just then. Because I missed Pacey, damn it. It had been less than a day since I saw him last, and I missed him. I had picked up my phone to text and call dozens of times since I walked out, but I hadn't, knowing he needed space. I would give it to him, even if it broke me in the process.

I wasn't very good at this. I didn't feel like I was good at anything lately, but I would try.

I made my way down the path and nearly ran into Sanders. He put his hands on my arms to steady me, and I gave him a slight nod before pulling away. His touch didn't revolt me as it probably should, but I didn't feel anything at the moment. The fact that I didn't, that I didn't really care at all, told me that maybe I was doing okay.

"You okay there?" Sanders asked, and I nodded tightly.

"Thanks for making sure I didn't fall. Bye."

He gave me a sad smile before walking away towards his new girlfriend. I walked the other way. I wasn't sad. I was over him. And later, I would think about that and relish the fact that maybe I was growing. But for now, I needed to get to my meeting and pretend that I wasn't in love with Pacey and breaking inside because I couldn't be with him.

I had so much else on my plate that I couldn't focus on Pacey. Or the fact that I missed him.

I made my way to Dr. Michaels' office and swallowed hard. I pushed my hair away from my face and tried not to look too disheveled. I knocked on the door.

"Come in," the man said in his gruff voice. I twisted the doorknob and walked inside.

Dr. Michaels gave me a grave look and gestured towards

the chair in front of him. "Take a seat. We have a few things to discuss."

"I'm glad I'm not late," Dr. Jackson said from behind me, and my eyes widened.

I frowned for a minute, wondering what this could be about as I looked between the two of them. Dr. Michaels narrowed his eyes at Dr. Jackson but gestured for her to take the other seat in front of his desk. Dr. Jackson gave me a small smile before she sat next to me. For some reason, I felt even more nervous, anxiety mixed with relief at seeing her.

"What's going on?" I asked.

"I suppose we'll have to explain it," Dr. Michaels said, his voice a growl.

Dr. Jackson cleared her throat. "Maybe I should do it," she said kindly. Of course, the look she gave Dr. Michaels could've cut someone to the quick so I didn't think the kindness was for him.

"Of course. Whatever. It's not like I have a say," he growled, and my eyebrows winged up.

Dr. Jackson cleared her throat. "It seems that one of our students was caught cheating and is facing expulsion. I can't explicitly tell you who, as that would be against the rules, but I can say that the internship and a program spot has opened up that I think you'll like."

I blinked at her, my chest tightening as I tried to absorb what she was saying.

"Who?" I asked and then shook my head. "Never mind. You just said you couldn't tell me who. Sorry. I mean, what internship are you talking about?"

"You know," Dr. Michaels growled. "The one you

applied for already. You'll be able to start this summer. And now that a certain student is no longer with us, you're going to be able to work with me as you wanted. Everything's working out for you, isn't it?" he asked, his tone bordering on petulant.

I blinked and looked at Dr. Jackson. "I don't understand."

She reached out and patted my hand for a moment before she leaned back again. "As I said, one of our students was caught cheating and is on academic probation, facing expulsion. What that means for you is that the spot you wanted before has now opened up." She met Dr. Michaels' gaze as he gestured for her to carry on. "However, I know that we discussed you possibly being able to work with another professor *and* me."

I blinked, trying to catch up. "I still don't understand," I said.

Dr. Michaels narrowed his eyes. "It's come to my attention that I *allegedly* nearly broke some ethics rules when I decided to work with the previous student. Now, the advisory board isn't sure they want you working with me alone."

I blinked and looked between them, suddenly having enough. Just...enough of everything. Of how I'd been treated. Of how this was going down now. Just...enough. "They're right," I said honestly, surprising myself and, apparently, Dr. Michaels.

"Excuse me?" he asked.

"I don't want to work with you," I said. "You lied to me and everyone else. You tried to ruin my academic career and most likely what comes after my bachelor's degree. All because you wanted the kid whose parents gave the school money. And while I'm probably shooting myself in the foot for even daring to say this, no, I don't want to work with you. You may be in the field that I want to be in, but you're not the only one. And it's taken me a long time to realize that I need to make my path and not follow the one I was set on at the beginning."

"You're saying you're just going to walk away after all of your complaining before?"

"Roger," Dr. Jackson snapped.

"What? She went to *how* many professors and tried to plead her case? And now she's just walking away? No, I don't believe it."

I shook my head. "You can believe whatever you want," I said honestly. "But, no, I don't want to work with you. This is my last semester with you anyway. My exam is already turned in. Anything I say to you right now can't hurt me. I'm sorry you had to change your plans, but you were rude to me. You lied and changed how I had to go about getting things done. You could have honestly hurt my chances of getting into the grad school I want. This next year, I'm going to do all that I can to make sure I can get in where I want and need, without using people who push me and throw me down when things get too tough."

"Good for you," Dr. Jackson said as she cleared her throat. "I have another option for you. Rather than you working with Dr. Linde, because I know that's not a field you're interested in at all, I want you to work with me."

I blinked. "I thought you didn't have space."

"Oh, we're going to make it work thanks to the open

spot with Dr. Michaels. The budget won't be a concern," she said.

"I don't understand," I said.

"We came to a decision that you were going to continue down the path you need to, and now, you're going to work with me. Dr. Michaels won't have a student this next year as he works on his papers and upcoming textbook. That leaves a spot open. We're going to make it work."

She talked again about logistics, and I felt like I was still trying to catch up. I felt lost and confused.

Hunter had cheated. And it had been bad enough that they'd had to do something about it. I didn't want to know the details because it wasn't my business, but somehow, it felt as if things were working out. I liked Dr. Jackson. She was basically who I wanted to be when I grew up, a joke I told myself often. And yet, she'd stood up for me, just like I was standing up for myself.

At the end of the meeting, I shook her hand, nodded at Dr. Michaels, and walked away, knowing that I had a plan to rework. One that would make sense. I wouldn't be behind. I wouldn't flounder.

I would thrive. On my own merits. And not just because they'd had to push me through.

I was practically beaming, even as I thought that I really wanted to talk to Pacey. Suddenly, I bumped into someone and looked up, only to swallow hard.

Hunter Williams, III looked down at me, his eyes narrowed. "You're happy, aren't you?" he asked.

"I'm sorry things didn't work out the way you wanted," I said honestly. Hunter was brilliant, but he was an asshole.

He tightened the hand on my forearm.

"You need to let me go," I said, alarm bells sounding in my head. He just narrowed his gaze.

"Oh, I do, do I? Who's going to stop me?"

I pulled away, twisting slightly, and he finally let go. "I don't know what's going on, but you need to leave me alone."

"You're going to be sorry you took my spot. My parents will fix this. And when they do, you'll never get into any program you want. My grandfather helped to build this department. He's still the most brilliant mind in our field. Do you think he'll just sit back and let a girl take my spot? No, you're going to regret this."

And then he stormed off, and I stood in the quad, wondering what exactly had just happened.

Hunter had been shaking, his face pale, his eyes bright. He was always an asshole, but he had never really threatened me like that before.

I rubbed my arm and knew I would likely have bruises later, but it didn't matter.

He was going away, would get kicked out of school. I needed to breathe.

"Mackenzie?"

I looked up as Pacey came toward me, his eyes narrowed, his jaw set.

"Pacey," I whispered. My heart raced at just the sight of him. His hair was disheveled, and he looked as if he were ready to hit someone.

And since he'd focused his gaze on where Hunter had gone, I had a feeling I knew who he wanted to hit.

"Did he hurt you?" he asked as he reached for my hand. He froze for a moment, then let his arm drop as if he were afraid to touch me.

I swallowed hard and then reached out to grip his hand. "Not really." I looked down at my arm. "Well, he sort of squeezed my arm, but it doesn't hurt." At least, not right then. I hoped it wouldn't later once the adrenaline was out of my system.

"Why would he do that? Why the hell am I not chasing him down and beating the shit out of him?"

I swallowed hard and looked up at him. "Apparently, he was caught cheating and was kicked out of the program. I got to take his spot for the internship." I explained everything, and the look in Pacey's eyes went from anger to excitement.

"Hell, yeah. I knew you were brilliant. And we're going to be working with the same professor."

I swallowed hard. "Is that okay? I know things are weird between us, and I just..." I took a deep breath. "I'm sorry for walking away yesterday. I thought it was what I was supposed to do."

Pacey cursed under his breath. "You did what you were supposed to, what you *needed* to do. Because I told you to. And because I was the asshole who pushed *you* away. I'm so damn sorry. I shouldn't have. Things just got confusing, and I didn't want to be the guy who put too much on your shoulders. But I ended up hurting you in the process. I'm so damn sorry."

I wiped a single tear from my face. "Don't...don't...let's just forget it."

He shook his head. "No, we're not going to forget it. I don't get to lash out and tell you to go away when things get hard. Yes, things are a bit insane right now, but I don't get to be that person." He took a deep breath and looked me in the eyes. My stomach clenched, and I licked my lips. "I love you, Mackenzie. I love you so fucking much. I know it's too soon. I know I was only supposed to be a rebound, but I'm not. I love you, and I'm sorry for hurting you."

I blinked and then moved forward, cupping his face in my hands. "I love you, too, Pacey. I know I wasn't supposed to fall for you because we didn't know what would happen in our futures. And as someone who needs to know those things, I figure this is probably a mistake, but I don't care. I love you, Pacey. Falling for you has been the most delightful and entangled thing I've ever done in my life, and I would do it again in a heartbeat. I left yesterday to give you space, but I'm not going anywhere. Not really."

"I went by your house to find you. Now, I'm here. I'll follow you to the ends of the Earth if you let me." And then he leaned down and brushed his lips against mine. My heart raced, and I wrapped my arms around his neck. People cheered, and I realized that I'd forgotten we were in public, but I ignored it all because I was falling more in love with my boyfriend—the guy who wasn't my rebound.

I pulled away and leaned my head against his. "Wow," I whispered.

He smiled against me. "Wow is a good thing."

He kissed me again, and then I looked over his shoulder as he leaned forward and frowned.

"You stupid bitch," Hunter shouted. "You don't get to take away my spot! My everything!"

I was so confused. Tried to let my mind catch up to what I was seeing. And then Pacey turned and blocked me.

I screamed as a metal glint and something in Hunter's

hands caught my eye as he came at us, and then Pacey pushed me to the ground. My head hit the concrete, I heard a loud sound, and then something warm slid over me. But there was no pain. Because Pacey blanketed me, and his face was pale. People were screaming.

And I shouted right along with them.

Twenty-Three

Pacey

"I'M FINE, MUM," I SAID AS I LEANED INTO THE pillow on my hospital bed. And it wasn't a lie. Hunter didn't have good aim, and I'd shoved my body over Mackenzie's just in time. I only had a small wound on my shoulder. The fact that the location of the graze meant that if I hadn't pushed Mackenzie out of the way soon enough, she'd have been hurt far worse wasn't lost on me. But it wasn't something I would think about. Not when I was on pain meds and trying to explain to my mother that I wasn't going to die.

"You say you're fine, but you were hurt," my mother said and shook her head. "I cannot believe you were shot. On campus."

"The shooter dropped the gun as soon as he fired," I said. "Campus security was there and took care of him."

Hunter had been taken away in handcuffs, sobbing. I had a feeling he'd had no idea that he was capable of something like that. It had surprised all of us, probably Hunter more so than anyone. Not that I had much pity for the guy. He had hurt me and tried to threaten and kill Mackenzie. It might've only been brandishing a threatening weapon to her, but he'd still fired.

The campus was on lockdown, even though it had been a single-shooter incident, and I didn't know when we would be able to go back. Or if we would at all. It was scary. I'd had to deal with questions from the police already, even after I'd had my arm bound.

I would have a scar, and thanks to my autoimmune disease, I would likely have to deal with an infection, but we were taking all the precautions. I would be in the hospital for a few days, longer than most people in my situation.

My mother had been by my side the entire time. I knew Mackenzie wanted to be, as well, but the authorities had questioned her even more than they did me. The same with the professors. It wasn't Mackenzie's fault. I would make sure she understood that, no matter what she thought.

Someone cleared their throat at the door, and I looked up to see my dad.

He was alone, no Jessica in sight, and I was grateful for that. Not that I didn't want to get to know my future sister whenever Jessica gave birth, but since Mum was here, I didn't want things to get more awkward.

"Pacey," my dad whispered before he looked at my mother. "I can come back."

Mum shook her head. "No, come in. It doesn't matter what's going on between us; we're still a family. And our son is sick. Standing together for him when he needs us is the one thing we were always good at." She gave Dad a small smile, and I saw the sadness there. I didn't know if I would ever forgive him for what he had done to her. I didn't know if I should or if it was even my place, but Mum was trying, and I supposed my dad was, as well.

"I'm not sure what to say," my dad said. "I can't believe you're here. That you were shot. On campus."

My chest hurt, and it had nothing to do with the shooting. My parents were here and ready to take care of me. That counted for a lot. I needed to get over my issues and remember that we'd been a family long before things changed so harshly. "I'm fine. My kidney is doing great. They're adding a bunch of stuff to my system to make sure an infection doesn't set in, and I'll only have a small scar."

"I want to wrap you in Bubble Wrap and take you back to England."

"I think my home is here now," I said and gave my dad a strained smile. "Is that okay?"

My mum wiped tears from her face. "We're okay with anything you want, Pacey. You're the one who's supposed to make the decisions. We're with you, no matter what." She met my dad's gaze as if threatening him to disagree with her.

My dad swallowed hard. "I agree with any decision you make. If you end up going to Oxford for a post-doc, though, you know you're always welcome. I'll be here and overseas both, depending on the month. I'm never leaving your life, Pacey, even if you want me to."

I sighed and sank into the pillows more. "I'm a little too

tired to have this conversation, but I don't want you out of my life. I just don't like you much right now."

My dad nodded tightly. "I don't blame you. I don't think I like myself much right now." He looked at my mum as he said it, and then he stuck his hands into his pockets. "I've made some mistakes, and I wanted to say I'm sorry."

My mum wasn't looking at him, but she smiled down at me, her hand in mine. I wasn't part of their marriage, and I wouldn't get in the middle of things, but my dad was here to check in on me, and that counted for something.

"We love you," my mom said. She looked at my dad, and he nodded. "And there is someone outside who wants to meet with you to talk. So, we're going to go. We'll see you tomorrow. You have an entire passel of roommates and girls out there wanting to speak with you. I think you'll be busy until it's time to rest. And you *will* rest." She squeezed my hand, and I smiled at her. "I love you, too. Both of you." I looked at my dad. "We'll talk later. I promise."

My dad gave me a tight nod, tapped my foot with his hand as if afraid to get too close, and gestured for my mom to lead him out. They left me alone for a few moments, and I wondered what would happen next. They weren't my responsibility, but I could love them, and I could try to figure out how they fit into my life. I couldn't fix my parents or make them love each other, but I could try to figure out who I was without them. And try not to fuck up my life with Mackenzie along the way.

And as if me thinking of her had brought her to me, Mackenzie stood in the doorway, her eyes wide.

"Mackenzie," I whispered.

She looked up at me and swallowed hard. "Pacey," she

breathed. And then she moved forward. She took a seat in the chair my mother had vacated and reached out as if to touch me. Only she froze, her eyes wide. "I don't know where to touch you. I don't know how I'm not going to hurt you."

Since she was on the side that I hadn't hurt, I reached out and gripped her hand, squeezing it hard. "I'm fine," I said. "I promise."

"You're lying. You were shot."

"I was grazed. You were almost shot."

Tears fell, and she leaned down and kissed my brow. "You saved my life," she whispered.

"Honestly, I think we saved each other. If you hadn't looked at him when you did and tried to push me out of the way, I wouldn't have known to turn."

"I don't even remember doing that."

"Well, you did. You saved me just as much as I saved you. And I never want to have to do anything like that again. We are never going to get into that kind of situation again."

She wiped away tears and kissed me softly on the mouth. "You're right. We're never doing that again. I love you so much, Pacey. I still can't believe Hunter did that."

I awkwardly reached for her with my good arm and brushed tears from her face. "I love you, too. And no, we're never letting that happen again. I'm never letting you go, Mackenzie. I don't know what will happen in the future or who we'll be, but I know whatever happens, I'll do it with you."

She smiled softly. "I wasn't expecting you, Pacey. But I should have." Then she kissed me softly, and I knew that we had far more things to worry about than each other at the moment. And we would.

We still had another year of school, and we had to deal with the fallout of what had just happened. And we would do that, too.

But for now, I moved over so she could join me on the bed, even if the nurses hated it, and then held the girl I loved close. I knew we could figure this out.

Because she would make her plans, and I would make sure they came to fruition.

I hadn't expected to fall in love with Mackenzie Thomas, and yet I knew it had been inevitable. It was meant to be from the first moment I saw her.

Even if she hadn't been mine at first and couldn't have been then. She was mine now. I smiled, knowing that this was the one rebound that would stick, no matter what.

Twenty-Four

Mackenzie

I SET OUT A VEGGIE PLATTER, AND TANNER frowned. "Where's the cheese? And the junk food? Why are you bringing broccoli to a house party?" he asked, though I knew he was only joking.

I rolled my eyes. "Because we need vegetables. They're good for you."

"So you say," he grumbled, though he did take a handful of cauliflower and carrots.

"If you want to keep that eight-pack or ten-pack or whatever-the-hell-pack you have past college, maybe you should eat healthier."

"I'm eating vegetables," he growled, and Miles laughed as he came forward. "Just snap peas. But they are the best." He grinned and took a handful.

"Well, apparently, if I just put random food in front of you, you'll eat it. And I don't have to worry about if it tastes good or not."

"We'll just judge you if it tastes bad," Tanner said as he shrugged, taking a bite of cauliflower.

"You'll do no such thing," Pacey said as he wrapped his arms around me. Well, his *arm*, his other one was still in a sling, though he was healing. School was over, and we were headed into our summer classes and internships next week. I still couldn't believe that Hunter had brought a gun onto campus and then actually fired it. I wasn't sure Hunter believed it either. Sanders and his family had even called to apologize for bringing Hunter into my life. I think they were as shocked as I was at what had happened.

Hunter was dealing with charges that I didn't want to think about and wouldn't return to school or his ordinary life ever again.

The university had shut down for the week after the incident, and people made up finals and labs and did what they had to do, though I knew some were getting by without it. It had been traumatizing, even if Pacey had been the only one who got hurt. I had hit my head, but I was fine. I still couldn't believe that Pacey had been shot saving my life.

Honestly, I couldn't believe a lot of what had happened.

We were having a house party now, something to end the semester with. Even though I knew that some kids had left campus soon after the shooting, I didn't know if they were coming back. It was a horrible thing, and I knew we'd all have to talk about it more, especially on the heels of losing Corinne. But we would. Because our group of eight was close.

Tonight, Dillon and Elise were in the corner, laughing with each other as they danced, but I wasn't sure they were even dancing to music. I had a feeling that Dillon would propose to Elise this next year, even if it felt like we were all too young. We weren't. People were getting married left and right at university, some even leaving to have children.

That wasn't part of my plan anytime soon, and I was cautious about making sure that didn't happen. But Pacey and I were together. He was my future, even if I didn't know what would happen after school. Because we were going to figure that future together. I'd found my path, but I didn't need a rebound or anything I had thought I needed at the beginning of the semester.

I only needed to find what worked for Pacey and me along the way. My biggest surprise.

This wasn't what I'd thought my future would be, but I was happy. Something I hadn't thought I could be without everything in place.

"You're looking all serious," Natalie said from my side. I looked over at her. She had her hair down and wore thick glasses tonight because her eyes had been itchy from allergies, and she didn't want to wear her contacts. She looked adorable—at least in my opinion. From the way some of the guys looked at her, I figured they probably thought she looked adorable, too. After all, she was wearing one of my shirts, her breasts a little bit bigger than mine, so they practically poured out.

She looked hot. Okay, so *not* adorable. And some of the guys clearly noticed.

Tanner and Miles were scowling at her, mostly because I had a feeling they felt like she was like their younger sister and were doing their best to protect her. At least, that's what I thought. For all I knew, I was as blind with them as I had been with Nessa, and something was secretly going on. Though I didn't think so.

Tanner left us and the vegetable tray to talk to his former duo, the man and woman he had been dating at the beginning of the semester. They didn't seem to be fighting, so I counted that as a win, though I still didn't know what was going on between those three. Tanner had said that he was single, but he sure looked hooked on them still.

Miles left us to go brood in the corner, and I didn't know what that was about.

Everybody had their issues. But I'd realized I didn't have to be the one to fix them all. I looked up at Pacey, who had noticed the same things I had. He wasn't trying to fix them either.

Nessa was absent tonight. I didn't know where she was, but at least fifty bodies were in this house. She had gone off dancing with another girl I knew from around campus, and I hadn't seen her since.

We were all getting along better, but it was still a bit awkward. I just hoped that we could work things out in the end. Pacey spun me in his arms as Natalie moved off to talk to someone, and I looked up at him.

"Hi there," I said.

He kissed me soundly, and someone cheered. "Hello there."

"You're looking mighty excited to be here."

"Oh, I am." He rubbed against me, and I felt the hard length of him press into me. I blushed, hoping nobody else saw.

We hadn't made love since before the shooting, but he had a clean bill of health now, so I had a feeling what we would be doing once everybody left.

Or if Pacey had his way, what we would be doing behind a closed door as soon as possible.

"Behave," I whispered.

"Never." He took my mouth again, and I sighed, feeling as if we were alone in the world.

I hadn't meant to fall for Pacey. I shouldn't have. I should have taken some time for myself and figured out who I needed to be. But I'd realized I could find myself at the same time I found a happily ever after. Something I hadn't thought about doing before.

I might not know exactly what the future held, but I knew who would be in it.

My plans would fall where they may later, and I would help them along, but I had Pacey by my side now. My favorite and only rebound.

My everything.

MILES

I scowled at another couple making out upstairs in the hallway, but I moved past them. They weren't in any of the bedrooms, and frankly, we'd probably have to bleach the whole area anyway. People were having a little too much fun tonight, and I was glad that we were kicking everybody out soon. I didn't mind house parties. I enjoyed hanging out with people, but this had been a long fucking semester, one with things I hadn't expected, and I just wanted people to go away. I needed to make sure the people I cared about were okay.

I turned the corner, headed towards my room, needing some space, and saw Nessa sitting on the floor, a bottle of wine in her hands as she leaned against the wall, her eyes closed.

I cursed under my breath, pissed off all over again. It might not have been Pacey's fault that he hadn't seen what his friend thought of him, but maybe it should be on him.

Perhaps Pacey should have gotten his head out of his ass and realized what he was doing to Nessa.

Because, Jesus, what the hell was I supposed to do for her now?

She was drunk, at a party, and in a short skirt. None of those things separately should matter, but I didn't trust anybody, and there were definitely some asshole predators out there. I sighed and knew I was about to make a really big fucking mistake, especially if she got mad at me for it. But I didn't care.

I moved forward and took the bottle from her hands. Her eyes widened, and she pouted up at me. "What was that for?"

"Come on, let's get you tucked in."

"I don't live here. And I'm not getting into anyone's bed." I pulled her to her feet, and she leaned into me, her legs wobbly. "I think I had too much to drink."

"Probably. But come on, I'll take care of you."

"Why? We're not friends, are we?"

I ignored the barb and unlocked my door. I walked her in and closed and locked the door behind us.

"We are. We just don't talk as much as I do with the others because you're friends with them more than you are with me."

"Maybe. Or maybe I'm such a bitch that I make people think they should feel sorry for me, but they shouldn't."

I shook my head and led her to the bed. "Let me get you some water."

She sat. "I'm fine. I just make stupid decisions and make people feel sorry for me, and I shouldn't. I need to be an adult. I have to be someone I like and respect. And I don't think I like myself right now."

I went to get her a bottle of water from my mini-fridge and handed it over to her after I unscrewed the top. "Drink."

"Yes, Daddy," she whispered.

I cringed. "Please don't call me that."

She chugged half of it and handed me the bottle back. "Thank you. I swear I'm not a bitch, but I feel like one lately. He was never mine, you know? He never was and won't be. But I got it into my head that maybe we could be something, and I acted all stupid about it."

I knelt in front of her and closed my eyes, then counted to ten. "We're allowed to be stupid about people we have crushes on."

"I thought I was in love with him."

"Maybe you were."

"No, if I were in love with him, he would've loved me back."

I shook my head. "I don't think that's how that works." She began to list a bit to the side, so I put my hands on her shoulders to keep her steady.

"You're going to be okay."

"What if I'm not?" she asked, looking at me. "What am I supposed to do?"

I pushed her hair away from her face and sighed. "Whatever you want to do."

She looked at me then and licked her lips. My gaze caught the movement, and I swallowed hard.

"Nessa."

She grabbed my shirt and pulled me towards her. Her

lips pressed against mine, and she tasted of sweetness and too much wine.

I pulled away and shook my head. "You're drunk. You don't know what you're doing."

"Probably not. Look at me, making another stupid decision." And then she leaned over and promptly fell asleep on my bed. I sighed and then slipped off her shoes. I tucked her in and knew it would be a long night.

"I wish you would remember this in the morning," I whispered.

Because she would forget. Much like she forgot every time she looked at me and right through me.7

I knew all about what it meant to have unrequited feelings.

After all, I lived with them every day.

****

Next in the ON MY OWN series?
Nessa and Miles figure out what they've been missing
in MY NEXT PLAY.

WANT TO READ A SPECIAL BONUS EPILOGUE FEATURING PACEY & MACKENZIE? CLICK HERE!

Bonus Epilogue

Pacey

"STRIP MATH IS NOT A GAME," MACKENZIE SAID, her hands on her hips. I leaned against the headboard, the book on my lap covering my erection. "Oh, I do believe it is."

"So, what? I get a question right, and I get to tell you to take off a piece of clothing?"

I raised a brow. "That works. However, the more questions I get correct, the more I get to take off your clothing. I do miss your nipples."

She blushed, and I grinned.

"Pacey."

"Don't *Pacey* me. You know I love your nipples."

She blushed. "Fine. I haven't seen you naked in...about an hour. It's time."

I laughed. "It's been since last night, you dork."

"You say that, but it's been too long," she said, pouting. I grinned and then kissed her soundly on the mouth.

"Okay, let's go."

I opened the textbook to the first question and asked it.

She got it right, of course, and then smiled. "Okay, I guess that means I get to take off a piece of your clothing."

My brows winged up. "Wait, is that what we're doing?"

"Fine, take it off. Let me see your nipples."

I laughed, leaned forward, and stripped my shirt off my body. I still had a bandage around my arm, but it was healing. Her gaze went to it, but it was okay. I'd have a scar, and we'd always remember that day, but it was the day I told her I loved her for the first time, so I would count that as a win.

"Again," she said, her gaze on my chest. I nearly flexed, but I held myself back.

I asked a more challenging question this time, and she was off by a single number as she looked up from her graph paper.

"That's it. Your shirt, too."

"But I'm not wearing a tank underneath. It's just my bra."

"Take it off. And if you resist too much, you're losing the bra, too. Come on. I need to see those nipples."

She laughed and slowly took off her shirt, letting it fall to the floor. My cock pressed hard against my zipper. I would be excited when she got another question right so I could take off my pants.

Slowly, question by question, we stripped each other, both laughing, even though I was so turned on I was ready to burst.

By the end of it, I was only in my boxer briefs, and she

was completely naked, scowling at me. "I think you're just making up math questions now."

"It's not my problem you can't concentrate." I rubbed myself through the fabric, and she groaned.

"I hate you."

"You are sitting naked on the edge of my bed, and I'm not touching you. I'm pretty sure I hate you right now for not being able to do so."

She pulled the book off my lap. Crawling towards me, her body naked and lithe, she straddled me. Her wet heat moved over me, and I groaned.

"So, is this how we're studying now?"

"I'm oddly delighted that you're not in any of my future classes." She moaned. "I'm never going to be able to concentrate again."

I tugged on her hair slightly and kissed her on the mouth. "You're right. We're going to have to study clothed in public because...any more of this? We're going to fail. But we'll be completely sated."

"It might be worth it."

She kissed me again, and then we were both laughing, wrestling.

Someone knocked on the door, and Mackenzie squealed before hiding under the blankets. We had already pulled off my boxer briefs, and I growled, tugging the blanket over my lap.

"What?" I growled through the door.

"We're having a house dinner," Tanner called from the hall. "Get your clothes on, or make it a quickie because everybody's here and we're waiting on you."

Mackenzie groaned into the pillow, and I sighed. "Give us twenty minutes."

"Make it five. If you can't get her off before then, there's something wrong with you."

He laughed as he walked away, and Mackenzie slowly reappeared from under the sheets. "I hate your roommates. I mean, I love them, they're like my brothers, but I hate them."

"I hate them, too. I guess we should get dressed."

She looked at me then, her smile going sly. "We have five minutes."

I grinned and then pounced.

As it turned out, we were late.

But I was just fine with that.

Just fine.

Thank you so much for reading!
Next up in the series: MY NEXT PLAY with Nessa and Miles.

A Note from Carrie Ann Ryan

Thank you so much for reading **MY REBOUND!**

This book took a deep dive into my own college years in science and math and all the while watching two people fall in love in their own way. I hope you loved them!

Next up in the ON MY OWN series?

Nessa and Miles aren't ready for what's about to hit them, but that's just fine. Nessa needs to heal and Miles has his own history. You can read their story in My Next Play!

The On My Own Series:

WANT TO READ A SPECIAL BONUS EPILOGUE

FEATURING **PACEY & MACKENZIE? CLICK HERE!**

If you want to make sure you know what's coming next from me, you can sign up for my newsletter at www. CarrieAnnRyan.com; follow me on twitter at @CarrieAnnRyan, or like my Facebook page. I also have a Facebook Fan Club where we have trivia, chats, and other goodies. You guys are the reason I get to do what I do and I thank you.

Make sure you're signed up for my MAILING LIST so you can know when the next releases are available as well as find giveaways and FREE READS.

Happy Reading!

ABOUT THE AUTHOR

Carrie Ann Ryan is the New York Times and USA Today bestselling author of contemporary, paranormal, and young adult romance. Her works include the Montgomery Ink, Redwood Pack, Fractured Connections, and Elements of Five series, which have sold over 3.0 million books worldwide. She started writing while in graduate school for her advanced degree in chemistry and hasn't stopped since. Carrie Ann has written over seventy-five novels and novellas with more in the works. When she's not losing herself in her emotional and action-packed worlds, she's reading as much as she can while wrangling her clowder of cats who have more followers than she does.

www.CarrieAnnRyan.com

ALSO FROM CARRIE ANN RYAN

The Montgomery Ink: Fort Collins Series:

The On My Own Series:

The Tattered Royals Series:

The Ravenwood Coven Series:

Book 1: Dawn Unearthed
Book 2: Dusk Unveiled
Book 3: Evernight Unleashed

Montgomery Ink:
Book 0.5: <u>Ink Inspired</u>
Book 0.6: <u>Ink Reunited</u>
Book 1: <u>Delicate Ink</u>
Book 1.5: <u>Forever Ink</u>
Book 2: <u>Tempting Boundaries</u>
Book 3: <u>Harder than Words</u>
Book 3.5: <u>Finally Found You</u>
Book 4: <u>Written in Ink</u>
Book 4.5: <u>Hidden Ink</u>
Book 5: <u>Ink Enduring</u>
Book 6: <u>Ink Exposed</u>
Book 6.5: <u>Adoring Ink</u>
Book 6.6: <u>Love, Honor, & Ink</u>
Book 7: <u>Inked Expressions</u>
Book 7.3: <u>Dropout</u>
Book 7.5: <u>Executive Ink</u>
Book 8: <u>Inked Memories</u>
Book 8.5: <u>Inked Nights</u>
Book 8.7: <u>Second Chance Ink</u>

Montgomery Ink: Colorado Springs
Book 1: Fallen Ink
Book 2: Restless Ink
Book 2.5: Ashes to Ink
Book 3: Jagged Ink

Book 3.5: Ink by Numbers

The Montgomery Ink: Boulder Series:
Book 1: Wrapped in Ink
Book 2: Sated in Ink
Book 3: Embraced in Ink
Book 4: Seduced in Ink
Book 4.5: Captured in Ink

The Gallagher Brothers Series:
Book 1: <u>Love Restored</u>
Book 2: <u>Passion Restored</u>
Book 3: <u>Hope Restored</u>

The Whiskey and Lies Series:
Book 1: <u>Whiskey Secrets</u>
Book 2: <u>Whiskey Reveals</u>
Book 3: <u>Whiskey Undone</u>

The Fractured Connections Series:
Book 1: Breaking Without You
Book 2: Shouldn't Have You
Book 3: Falling With You
Book 4: Taken With You

The Less Than Series:
Book 1: Breathless With Her
Book 2: Reckless With You
Book 3: Shameless With Him

The Promise Me Series:
Book 1: Forever Only Once
Book 2: From That Moment
Book 3: Far From Destined
Book 4: From Our First

Redwood Pack Series:
Book 1: An Alpha's Path
Book 2: A Taste for a Mate
Book 3: Trinity Bound
Book 3.5: A Night Away
Book 4: Enforcer's Redemption
Book 4.5: Blurred Expectations
Book 4.7: Forgiveness
Book 5: Shattered Emotions
Book 6: Hidden Destiny
Book 6.5: A Beta's Haven
Book 7: Fighting Fate
Book 7.5: Loving the Omega
Book 7.7: The Hunted Heart
Book 8: Wicked Wolf

The Talon Pack:
Book 1: Tattered Loyalties
Book 2: An Alpha's Choice
Book 3: Mated in Mist
Book 4: Wolf Betrayed
Book 5: Fractured Silence
Book 6: Destiny Disgraced
Book 7: Eternal Mourning

Book 8: <u>Strength Enduring</u>
Book 9: <u>Forever Broken</u>

The Elements of Five Series:
Book 1: From Breath and Ruin
Book 2: From Flame and Ash
Book 3: From Spirit and Binding
Book 4: From Shadow and Silence

The Branded Pack Series:
(Written with Alexandra Ivy)
Book 1: <u>Stolen and Forgiven</u>
Book 2: <u>Abandoned and Unseen</u>
Book 3: <u>Buried and Shadowed</u>

Dante's Circle Series:
Book 1: <u>Dust of My Wings</u>
Book 2: <u>Her Warriors' Three Wishes</u>
Book 3: <u>An Unlucky Moon</u>
Book 3.5: <u>His Choice</u>
Book 4: <u>Tangled Innocence</u>
Book 5: <u>Fierce Enchantment</u>
Book 6: <u>An Immortal's Song</u>
Book 7: <u>Prowled Darkness</u>
Book 8: Dante's Circle Reborn

Holiday, Montana Series:
Book 1: <u>Charmed Spirits</u>
Book 2: <u>Santa's Executive</u>
Book 3: <u>Finding Abigail</u>

* 9 7 8 1 6 3 6 9 5 4 5 7 8 *